Next to Mexico

By Jennifer Nails

Houghton Mifflin Company
Boston 2008

This book is dedicated to Sasha Domnitz and Julie Stainer, who have believed in Lylice and Mexico from the very beginning.

www.houghtonmifflinbooks.com

The text of this book is set in Bookman BT.

Library of Congress Cataloging-in-Publication Data
Nails, Jennifer.
Next to Mexico / by Jennifer Nails.
p. cm.
Summary: Outspoken, impulsive Lylice has skipped fifth grade, but she finds that getting along at Susan B. Anthony Middle School is more difficult than she expected, until she befriends another newcomer to the sixth grade.
ISBN-13: 978-0-618-96635-6
[1. Friendship—Fiction. 2. Interpersonal relations—Fiction. 3. Middle school—Fiction. 4. Schools—Fiction. 5. Mexican Americans—Fiction. 6. Arizona—Fiction.] I. Title.
PZ7.N1388Ne 2008
[Fic]—dc22
2008007268

Manufactured in the United States of America
MP 10 9 8 7 6 5 4 3 2 1

Contents

A Magic Elevator of Her Own

I will never go to fifth grade. I got to skip it. It is as if I took an elevator up from fourth, and everyone else took the stairs. At first I liked the idea. But that was in the spring, when Principal Garrison told my parents and me. I got to wonder about what sixth grade might be like while still in the normalness of fourth grade.

School started on the Tuesday after Labor Day. Principal Harrington called me into his office before first period.

"You're kidding me," he barked into the phone. I waved. He shot out of his seat and glared at me. "No. No. There *isn't* still time to find someone else. Marcia, it's the first day of school and I need you here!"

I stood in his doorway, waiting. Last night he'd called my parents and told them I should come talk to him first thing in the morning. He'd said to. What was I supposed to do? On his desk, a half-eaten blueberry muffin sat on stacks and stacks of file folders. The office was a tiny rectangle, but Principal Harrington didn't take up much space.

I had worried about sixth grade all summer. Not the school part of it—the friend part. In fourth grade I was best friends with Principal Garrison. She turned sixty-five in May. They had a party for her but I wasn't invited. In third grade I got to know the librarian, Miss Phillips, really well, because I was always in there. She lived with her sister, Maude, and they took care of their old mother. But let's just put it this way: you can't invite a real grown woman over for a sleepover.

"Well, fine, then. Go to Cherryvale. You know they don't need you there like we need you here, Marcia!" he shouted. "And don't expect a recommendation from me!" He slammed down the phone. "Argh," he growled.

I took one step back and attempted to tiptoe out

the door. I'd come back later.

"Lie-lice Martin," he said, snatching the blueberry muffin and hurling it into the trash. "Welcome. Mrs. Garrison has told me all about you." He flopped into his seat and started rubbing his forehead, smiling a little. "We're both glad you're here."

"Thank you, Principal Harrington," I said. "Sorry your first day of school isn't going so well."

His smile got bigger but it seemed like the feeling behind it got smaller.

"I'm glad I'm here, too," I said quickly. But I wished it wasn't happening yet. I wished there was time for more wondering and dreaming about what sixth grade might be like. And I wished his day wasn't going so badly, because he was making me want to be back at Catalina Foothills Elementary School with Mrs. Garrison, not here with him at Susan B. Anthony Middle School.

"You wanted to see me?" I asked.

Through the whole conversation we had about striving for excellence, he opened and slammed drawers, flipped through folders, and scribbled on Post-Its. He called me Lie-Lice three times. Finally I said: "It's

3

*Lyli*ce. Like *Phyllis.*" I said I'd been called worse. He didn't laugh. But he did tell me to come in and visit whenever I wanted. I was not sure I would.

My very first class of sixth grade was Spanish. Señora Schwartz had us pick a Spanish name that we would go by for the entire year. I considered all of the choices on the board. But I wanted something that sounded fancy and different.

"Concepción," I said, when it was my turn. I used my best Spanish accent, putting emphasis on the *ión* part of the word. Señora raised her eyebrows and said: "*Interesante!*" I smiled.

Two girls and a boy with black curly hair burst out laughing. Then they all put their top teeth over their bottom lips and stared at me. I squashed my lips shut. I knew those three. They had been in fifth grade at Catalina Foothills Elementary last year. Tony Frizell, Hannah Anderson, and Debbie Dominguez.

I knew why they were sticking their teeth out like that. Everyone did that to me last year, too. Instead of pointing down at my bottom lip, like they're supposed to, my two front teeth point *out*.

Suddenly, Señora's door flew open. Heads turned

4

toward it. Principal Harrington and a short girl walked in. A *very* short girl. And skinnier than a baby puppy. She was clutching pink backpack straps. Señora shook her hand and said *hola*. After patting the girl's shoulder and whispering something to Señora, Principal Harrington left.

"*Estudiantes,* say *hola* to Mexico Mendoza," said Señora.

Before I could think, before I could not think, I stood from my chair.

"*Hola,* Mexico!" I said, alone. I grinned at her from my desk, my two front teeth almost stretching the distance between us to shake her hand.

My class burst out laughing. I fell back into my seat and chewed my lip. People kept giggling. Mexico Mendoza smiled at me and sort of waved. I waved back with pursed lips, a smile bubbling inside of me. She wore a flowered dress and white straw sandals. It seemed as though she had taken a magic elevator to get here too.

Señora pointed her toward the empty desk next to me.

"Hi, I'm Lylice," I whispered, putting my hand out.

5

"That's *L-y-l-i-c-e*. Lylice." Mexico shook my hand and sat down. I liked her red butterfly barrettes.

At the end of class, Señora assigned me to be Mexico's English Buddy for the year, since our last names were right next to each other, Martin and Mendoza. Mexico had a good smell. Like vanilla and . . . maybe strawberries.

In Mrs. Lanza's class, I volunteered to write for the *Suffragette Star*. In Coach's class, I signed up for tennis. And Mr. Schvitter had class-president candidate sheets for those interested. I took one. Get in on the action, my dad had said. I was. But so far my only friend was turning out to be my brain-on-wheels. My dad gave our old rolling carry-on suitcase the name. It was the only thing big enough for all of my supplies.

If only suitcases could talk. And laugh. And understand you. And guide you through Ballot Hall, where everyone else knows one another and looks at you. I was determined to make friends with someone under forty-five this year.

After school, I found Mexico standing outside Principal Harrington's office.

"I think we have all our classes together!" I said. I didn't mean to sound so excited about it.

She nodded. Her shoulder-length black hair covered half of her face, and she peered at me with one eye. She held her backpack straps in tight fists.

"You going in to talk to the head honcho?" I gestured grandly to his nameplate: PRINCIPAL CORNELIUS HARRINGTON III.

Mexico nodded and smiled. It made me feel brave. "I think I'll say hi too," I said. I was sure that he would be in a better mood than he had been before school. It was the end of the day. Everybody was in a good mood at the end of the day.

Principal Harrington's voice floated through his slightly open door. We knocked, but he didn't answer. So we peeked in.

Since his back was to us, we could see the hem of his plaid suit jacket unraveling. There were these pink slips on his desk that said TRANSFER REQUEST. We didn't mean to listen, but we did.

"I'm looking for any cuts I can make," he said into the telephone. "Now, isn't there any way you can take her back?"

Take *who* back?

"I know what I said, Esmeralda," he said.

I grabbed Mexico's arm. I didn't mean to. "Esmeralda is the name of my old principal at my last school," I whispered. "Esmeralda Garrison."

Ballot Hall was noisy with the whole school leaving for the day. Boys were yelling and girls were squealing. Harrington continued.

"I don't think it's unethical. Esmeralda, I'm stuck here. My secretary just quit on me, I just got another foreign student, and I have several sixth-grade repeats this year. More than usual. Now, can't we just tell her parents that it's not working out, that Lie-lice is not meeting our standards . . ."

I chewed my bottom lip. Would he really lie to my parents and tell them I wasn't meeting standards? Wasn't that against the law? School hadn't even really started yet. Preposterous.

On the last day of fourth grade, I gave Mrs. Garrison a baby frog. She collects them. It wasn't cheap, but my dad helped out. She also has chinchillas, hamsters, and mice. She was the best principal in the world. Last year at parent-teacher conferences,

Principal Garrison told my parents she thought I was extraordinary. And that I had potential. Now, after a whole summer of wondering and getting excited about sixth grade, was I going to be sent back to fifth?

I have started to question my extraordinariness.

Swellby Shelby

"Lilac, rose, or amaryllis, no one smells as good as Lylice! Lilac, rose, or amaryllis, no one smells as good as Lylice!" I chanted at the front of the gym. It was Friday morning. Presidential elections. I needed to win. I needed to prove to Principal Harrington that I would be able to meet standards, get friends, and fit right in.

Candidates were allowed to do some campaigning before Art Attack. A yummy smell filled the gym. Two tables down, Gorpat Geetha was giving away mini egg rolls with a choice of three sauces. His posters said GORPAT'S BACK! Gorpat was the smartest boy in seventh grade.

"Lilac, rose, or amaryllis," I yelled.

"No one stinks as bad as Lylice!" sang Tony Frizell, who came up to my table with a huge mob of kids behind him. My face felt hot. I was not in the mood for insults.

"Hey, Stinky, we all want to vote for you. Can we have our cookies?" Tony asked.

"Sure," I said, handing them out as fast as people could take them. "Lilac, rose, or amaryllis. No one smells as good as Lylice!" I yelled and yelled. "Presidential elections are today, sixth period! Vote for Lylice!"

"Whatever, Walrus," Tony said, biting into his cookie. "No one knows what the freak you're saying. What the heck's am-a-rylla-blah-blah-blah . . . ?"

"They're flowers," said Sari Henderson, a pretty, black eighth-grade girl who stood behind a table next to me, passing out buttons that said SIMPLY PUT: SARI'S THE BEST. I was wearing one. "Get it, Tony? She's passing out *flower*-shaped cookies?"

"Whatever," said Tony.

Sari shook her head. "Good luck, Lylice," she said.

"You, too," I said. I hoped so hard that I'd win sixth-grade class president and Sari'd win eighth.

It would be tough. My opponent was Nathan Shelby. On the other side of the gym, kids, mostly girls, crowded around a table with a poster that said SWELLBY SHELBY. I could not let his popularity stop me.

There was a *tap tap tap* on my shoulder.

"Need help?" asked Mexico Mendoza.

"Yes! Thank you," I said.

I felt like I kept giving cookies to the same people over and over. In about thirty seconds, Mexico and I passed almost all of them out. Hannah and Debbie came back and got another.

"Hola," Mexico said, looking at Debbie.

"Hola," Debbie said to the floor. She spoke so quietly that baby mice wouldn't have heard. Hannah whispered something to Debbie, and they smirked at each other. I wanted to punch them both.

"Hey, Frizell," someone said in a low voice. It was Mike Black, who was suddenly standing on the other side of me, behind the table.

Mike was the meanest boy in school. And he was even taller than some eighth graders. Not just tall, but big all over. He always carried a camouflage

12

knapsack, and he had a ponytail. Mike was repeating sixth grade this year.

"What?" said Tony.

"You're gonna vote for her, right?"

"Yeah, Injun, I am. Now leave me alone, jerk." Kids were frozen, staring from Tony to Mike with their mouths full of cookie.

"Watch your filthy mouth," said Mike.

"Tony, off with you," I said. "You've had like three cookies already. Let some other people have theirs."

"Shut up, Walrus," said Tony. He tossed a cookie at me. But instead it hit Mike Black in the neck. A few kids laughed, but mostly people just stared or said, "Oooooooh." Principal Harrington's whistle blew. Most kids, including me, covered their ears. I noticed Mexico didn't.

"Excuse me," Harrington said, breaking through the clump of students. "What's going on here?" Once he saw Mike Black, he walked over and took him by the arm. "Black, come with me," he said.

"But Black didn't do anything," I said. "Tony Frizell said—"

"Lie-lice, now, just mind your own business," Harrington said. Mike followed him past everyone, all the while staring Tony down and mouthing something to him. Tony shrugged his shoulders and made a face, but I thought I saw him shudder. The whole scene broke up and the campaigning ended. It was time for art.

The theme for our very first Art Attack was "A Summer Memory." You were supposed to paint or draw something that had happened to you over the summer. Even though I was nervous about the election and I couldn't get Tony Frizell's mean comment to Mike Black fully out of my mind, Art Attack was fantastic. There were supplies on all these long tables. Stacks of all different colored construction paper. Paints, markers, and crayons in little containers, and tiny bottles of glue and glitter and stickers.

I couldn't find Mexico anywhere, so I chose a table right in the front of the gym. Nathan Shelby and some other sixth-graders were already sitting there. "Can you please pass that turquoise-y color?" I asked Nathan.

"Turquoise-y?" he asked, shaking his head. "Lylice, you weirdo." He paused from outlining his lion and set the paint next to me. Nathan was my ride to school. He was a year older than me, but now we were both in sixth grade. We had lived next door to each other, on Saguaro Circle, since I was born.

He grinned at me when he caught me looking at his lion, which was standing by a tree. I smiled back. For some reason, my face felt hot. I liked being called a weirdo.

"Did you meet a lion this summer or something?" I asked.

Nathan laughed. "Well, uh, we didn't have a conversation, but I did see one at the San Diego Zoo."

I giggled.

"Nate, come sit by us," said Tony, who sat at the other end of the table with Hannah and Debbie.

"Pleeeeeese," said the girls. They all had their top teeth hanging over their bottom lips.

"I'm fine here," said Nathan. They wouldn't stop with the teeth business. I kept my eyes on my drawing of Meatball. I finished painting her body and went to work on her eyes. Nathan sighed and stood up, took his lion, walked over, and plopped into a chair next to Tony.

15

I guessed Nathan wasn't really my *friend*. He was just a boy I'd known for a long time. He didn't *have* to sit near me. But why didn't he stay put? There was something brewing inside me, but dotting turquoise paint into Meatball's eyes looked and felt just right.

"Walrus got left all alone, huh? Poor Walrus," said Tony, grabbing the edge of the table with both hands and making it wobble. The paper cups of water shook and barely stayed up.

I pretended I didn't hear him. I dabbed my brush into the gray and made more streaks in Meatball's fur. "Walrus" was a name I'd hoped to leave behind at Catalina.

"Walrus got left all by herself," Tony said, shaking the table some more, trying to make me mess up. I slammed down my brush.

"For your information, my name is *Lylice*," I said. "Capital *L*, *y-l-i-c-e*. Lylice."

Tony and the girls turned into hyenas. Nathan just kept painting a strip of blue at the top of his lion scene. Tony shook the table harder.

"Quit," said Nathan. Tony quit.

Mexico came and sat right next to me. "Oh, hi," I said. "You're supposed to draw something that you did over the summer. Or paint. Whichever you want." She nodded and dipped a brush into the yellow.

Tony started shaking the darn table again.

Sploosh.

A cup of rinse water and brushes tipped over, right onto my painting.

"Darn it, Tony Frizell," I said, standing up and glaring at them. They roared even louder. "You people are exasperating!"

"Oops, sorry, Walrus," said Tony. He stood up, and the girls followed him, all three of them sneering at me with their imitation buckteeth. They walked off to another table. Mexico followed them.

"Preposterous!" I said.

Nathan Shelby sat with his head down, painting his name at the bottom of his picture. Mexico came back with a tissue. She pressed on my painting in all the places where it had gotten wet. Then she held it up.

"It was supposed to be my cat," I said, sinking into my seat. Because of the spill, Meatball's fur now looked all puffed out, like how cats get when they're spooked.

"Maybe it's your cat . . . that just saw Tony Frizell," she said. We giggled. Mexico Mendoza knew the right things to say. I glanced at her painting. It was a white bus going along this zigzaggy trail in the desert.

"Mexico . . . that's good," I said. "That's genius. Wow." It was. Everyone was looking twice at Mexico's art. I wished we could have Art Attack every morning, not just on Fridays.

I was anxious all through the rest of school. Sixth period finally came. Harrington got on the PA system. Miss McGriff, our band teacher, rolled her eyes and put down her baton.

"Greetings, students," Harrington's voice said. "It's time to exercise your right to vote. Your sixth-period teachers will now pass out your ballots. Show your Trailblazer pride and vote for the candidate who you think is best. Good luck to all. Thank you."

THE SUFFRAGETTE STAR

VOLUME 1

TOSS ME A MELODY
by Lylice Martin, Staff Writer

Being in the Jewel of the Desert Trailblazer band is like being in a salad of music.

I, the French horn, am the tomato. A really rich, red sound. Mexico Mendoza, our tuba, is the onion, because she makes such a heavy, blatting noise. Percussion (Danny Gonzales, Michelle Clark, and Cindie Disalvo) is the lettuce, keeping things together with a beat. You can chop in clarinets for carrots (Rosie Alfieno, Beebee Becker, Lisa Brown, and Rory Perkins), because they play all those little fast notes. For trombones (Nathan Shelby and Tony Frizell), let's slide in some blue cheese dressing because their sound gets poured out. Don't forget the saxophones (Will and Mark Wesley, and Debbie Dominguez), because they are the croutons that get trilled onto the meal. And sprinkle some flutes (Ana Goffmeier, David Sharp, May Cass, and Sari Henderson) as bacon bits because their parts are at the top.

Ms. McGriff gets to toss us every afternoon from 1:35 to 2:10.

Yum!

The Buffoon

On Monday, when we were just about to run through "Lightly Row," Principal Harrington came on the PA system. Miss McGriff slammed her baton on her podium. He announced everything so fast, I didn't even have time to get nervous.

Sari Henderson was the new eighth-grade class president. Gorpat won for seventh. And Swellby Shelby was the new sixth-grade class president.

Not me.

"Leelas," said Mexico as we walked together down the Ballot Hall steps after school. I didn't answer her. "I'm sorry," she said, taking her painting of the bus out of her backpack. "You said you liked it. Here," she said.

I smiled but couldn't say anything. I took her painting and hugged it to my chest. I just kept thinking of the eggs my mom had bought for all those cookies. And the sprinkles. And the cooking oil. Mexico walked across the Great Lawn and got into a black truck.

I went to bed early that night. I said I had studying to do. Meatball purred me to sleep. In the morning I felt a little better. After all, I was the proud owner of one of Mexico's masterpieces.

"Well, Miss Lylice," Mr. Shelby said when he dropped us off at school on Tuesday morning. "The buffoon doesn't deserve it, but I hope you'll give Mr. President here a hand if he needs it."

"Sure," I said. "If he needs it."

"Oh, mark my words, he will. I don't know what happened with this one," said Mr. Shelby, whapping the back of Nathan's head gently with his palm. "Scott and Sean didn't need as much extra attention as *he* does!"

But Nathan's brothers always *got* more attention than he did. And his stepmoms always got more attention than any of them. He'd had three different stepmoms, and they had each redecorated the Shelbys' house. All of them had completely different taste.

Mr. Shelby's cell phone ring tone was the first few bars of Beethoven's Fifth Symphony, the scary symphony with the four angry-sounding notes right in the beginning. Mr. Shelby clicked his earpiece. "This is Stuart Shelby," he said. "Oh, Sandy. Hi."

From the back seat, I caught Nathan's eye in the rearview mirror. He rolled his eyes. Then he smiled at me. I could feel my cheeks getting warm.

Nathan's dad looked just like Nathan, only in man form. At parent-teacher events, teachers always talked to Mr. Shelby for longer than they talked to other parents, especially female teachers. And they always seemed to be laughing at something he had just said. He looked sort of like a movie star, with brown-blond hair and these bright blue eyes. He was tall, too. With perfect teeth.

"Well, you know what, Sandy," said Mr. Shelby. "Thanks, but I'm going to pass. I had a good time last night too. But . . . I'm just"—he glanced down at Nathan—"going to pass."

Of all the boys to lose to: Nathan Shelby. Once, on a camping trip, we waded together in the mud in our underwear. There are photos to prove it.

Dear Nathan,

Congratulations on your presidency. If you need help, I can help, if I'm not too busy.

W/B/S (means write back soon),

Lylice

P.S. I was *not* staring at you during my thirty-two-measure rest.

P.P.S. *Don't* show this to anyone.

Mexico Says Yes

"Leelas, I don't know," said Mexico.

"Come on, I read you mine," I said. We were working on our My Favorite Place essays for Mrs. Lanza's class. We sat at the top of the Ballot Hall steps, waiting for our rides.

"Okay," she said, patting her hair over her ear. "I need help. But no laughing," she said.

"Never," I said. She looked down at her essay, which sat in her lap. Three big eighth-grade boys banged through the door of Ballot Hall and trampled down the stairs, hollering.

Mexico looked behind her to make sure no one else was coming. She cleared her throat and held up the paper.

"Okay. 'My Favorite Place.'" She cleared her throat again. "'My favorite place is a place where there is someone I love. For example, if my father is at a place, like my house in Nogales, that is my favorite place. Or another example would be the place where my dog, Pocho, is. That is my favorite place. Or my auntie. If she is at a place, that is my favorite place. A favorite place means who is there, instead of where it is.'"

Mexico made a face.

"Mexico." I leaned in to her. "That was genius," I said. "Holy moly, you're a great writer."

"Really?" asked Mexico.

"Really," I said. "You should write for the newspaper."

"I don't know," she said, shaking her head. "Maybe . . . but not yet."

"Well, you should think about it. Anyhow, let me see. There are just a few small things . . ." She handed me her paper. It was very easy to fix some of the grammar.

"Thanks, Leelas," she said, grinning. I nodded.

"You know," I said, "AIMS tests are in February.

As your English Buddy, I think it's my duty to have you over to study."

AIMS stood for Arizona's Instrument to Measure Standards. It was weird that the words *instrument* and *measure* were describing these huge, boring tests, and not band. There were never any music or art questions, or even a social studies section. My dad said that AIMS was a bunch of hooey.

"Yes, I want to come over," said Mexico, pointing to a black truck and pulling on her backpack. We stood up and started down the steps.

"How about this weekend?" I asked. Mexico nodded.

"I think so," she said. "Yes."

"That's great," I said, trying to sound normal. She was coming over! Once, I asked Miss Phillips if she wanted to come over and watch the eclipse with me. She said she had tickets to the ballet. I like to give her the benefit of the doubt about whether she really had those tickets.

We walked across the Great Lawn to where kids got picked up. Mike Black stood really close to Tony Frizell, whose back was pressed against a tree. I heard Mike say *ever again,* and then he stalked away. I almost felt sorry for Tony. He didn't *mean* to hit the biggest boy in school with a cookie.

Mexico's truck was scratched. The rust-colored passenger door was obviously from another truck. Her mother was talking to Hannah Anderson's mother through the driver's-side window. With her head down, Mexico opened the door and climbed in.

I didn't mean to, but I stared at Mrs. Anderson when she left because she was walking funny. I thought she might fall, but she didn't. She opened the door of a fancy blue car and got in. Hannah was waiting in the passenger seat.

Other kids were staring too. It wasn't just me. Was Mrs. Anderson sick? And why was Mexico's mother talking to her? Were Hannah and Mexico becoming friends?

"*Hola,* Mrs. Mendoza," I said, waving.

"*Hola.* You must be Leelas. I'm Maria," she said. "I'm Mexico's *auntie.* I have heard all about you." Mexico's cheeks went red. For the first time in my life, I liked having someone mispronounce my name.

Lylice Martin

Room 3A

Mrs. Lanza, English Language Arts

My Favorite Place Assignment

Bear Mountain

My favorite place is Bear Mountain, elevation 6,000 feet. On the way up the mountain you can see forests of saguaro cactuses. Some are thirty feet tall. They look like friendly giants with their thick arms waving out of their fat trunks. But don't try and hug one, because prickles all over their bodies keep kangaroo rats from eating holes in them.

From the top of Bear Mountain, you are half terrified and half electrified, all in one. You might fall because you're so high up. You can see Mexico from up there. I think it is quite remarkable to be able to look smack-dab at another country with your very own eyes.

You feel like a star, being up so high and looking down on everything. It is definitely

Late for Lunch

The whole school stood on the empty gym floor on Friday morning, jabbering. I knew there were seven hundred students at our school because that was how many copies Mrs. Lanza made of the *Suffragette Star* every other week.

Art Attack stations weren't set up. The bell rang, and Principal Harrington rushed in. He blew his whistle three times to get everyone quiet. When he started speaking, there were still murmurs and whispers coming from different pockets of kids in the gym.

"Excuse me. I need your attention. Now, students, we've had to make some new arrangements," he yelled, standing under the basketball hoop. "Art Attack is cut for the present."

how stars feel, being so far away from each other up there. Even though they are billions of light-years away from one another, they are all still stars, all still up there together. Stars wonder if there is another star just like them somewhere. On Bear Mountain, you pretty much feel like there is.

What? But we had only had Art Attack one time! Preposterous.

"Bone!" Tony Frizell yelled.

"Double bone!" I shouted. Kids looked back at me.

"Students, please head to your first-period classes, which you'll report to on Friday mornings from now on," Harrington yelled.

"Art At-tack! Art At-tack! Art At-tack!" I chanted, alone. I wondered where Mexico was. Debbie and Hannah glared at me.

"Har-ring-ton! Is-a-hack! Har-ring-ton! Is-a-hack!" a boy shouted, stomping his feet in rhythm. It was Mike Black, on top of the bleachers. Other boys were climbing up to join him. Soon, most of the school was yelling and stamping. Even Hannah and Debbie!

Harrington's whistle blew. Once. Twice. We chanted louder.

"Har-ring-ton! Is-a-hack! Har-ring-ton! Is-a-hack!" we all screamed. We were all in on the action! We were overcoming! Changing the world! Harrington waved his arms in the air and blew his

whistle again, this time so loud that my ears pinched in pain. We all gradually stopped.

"You," he yelled, pointing to the bleachers. "Black! Down. Now! Or you're *toast,* my man!" Harrington blotted his forehead with a tissue. "Everyone get to your classes!"

He flung open the door to Ballot Hall. Everybody filed out. I looked around for Mexico. I saw Mike and his friends slip out the side door of the gym, which led to an alley in back of the school.

Great. No more art. No more of the best part of the week. My second article in the *Suffragette Star* was due on Monday. I'd write all about Art Attack being canceled. I'd say that students were angry. And that maybe the school could come up with a plan to bring it back.

In English, Mrs. Lanza handed back our My Favorite Place essays. I got a B–. She wrote, *Fun imagery,* but at the end she said, *A bit disjointed. I know you can do better!* What if I couldn't? I was supposedly a straight-A student. Bone. Maybe Mr. Harrington was right about me. Maybe I couldn't meet standards.

"Sweet children, look to the back bulletin board,"

said Mrs. Lanza. Everyone turned around. Instead of the orange WELCOME BACK sign she had up before, there were five papers hanging there over a purple background.

She went on. "If you are not holding on to your essay right now, it's because your stellar A paper is on display," said Mrs. Lanza. "Now, welcome to the wonderful world of poetry . . ." She went on about haiku and limericks.

People looked around the room to see who was holding their essay and who wasn't. Nathan Shelby was looking at his folded hands and turning red. I glanced at Mexico, whose dimples were huge and deep. She looked at me and held up her empty hands! I gave her two thumbs-up. I was so proud, but jealous.

Shame flooded through me as she approached me in the cafeteria later that day. I'd chosen a red table in the corner. Mexico always had to go to the bathroom right before lunch, so she came in a little late.

"I cannot believe it," she said. "My first English A."

"Yes, Mexico. Very well deserved."

"Thank you, English Buddy," she said. For a second I thought she would cry. "Thank you for help."

It dawned on me. Someone had wanted my help, so I had helped, and it had paid off. But it wasn't just any someone. Sure, I had helped people I didn't know before, like when Miss Phillips and Maude and I volunteered at the soup kitchen on Thanksgiving. But helping a someone I *did* know was different. The jealousy was still there, but it was going away.

"You're welcome," I said, smiling at her. "This is not the only A you will get this year if I have anything to do with it!" I pounded the table.

Mexico was already meeting standards, and she had just learned English. I wondered if she ever wished she were in a school with ESL classes, English as a Second Language. There were some in Tucson. I hoped not.

"Hey, are you okay?" I asked. "You were late this morning. And late for lunch again."

"Yes. I'm okay," she said.

"Good," I said. I glanced over at the yellow table. Hannah, Debbie, and Nathan were laughing really loud while Tony Frizell dumped his water bottle all over his lunch tray. All of a sudden, Principal Harrington and Señora Schwartz were walking toward us. My heart started to thump in my chest.

"Uh-oh," I said. It was over. He was going to ask to talk to me privately, then tell me he had to send me back to fifth grade. That's what he'd told Mrs. Garrison that day, and—

"Hi, girls," he said with a smile.

"Hola, señoritas," Señora said, pulling up a chair. "Principal Harrington and I wanted to talk to both of you about Mexico's diabetes."

I sat up straight. "Oh, sure. Okay," I said. Mexico looked down. Diabetes? Winnie Mandela has diabetes. I did a report on her in third grade. It has to do with eating sugar.

Mexico's cheeks were pink and she stared at her carrots. Mr. Harrington said that diabetes was not serious if it was treated properly.

"We just thought her English Buddy should know," said Señora, winking at me. "Mexico, and if you can't find an adult, you let Concepción know if you're ever not feeling well, okay?" Mexico nodded. "And Concepción, you keep a good eye on her. As long as she is taking her insulin before lunch every day, she'll be just fine, okay?"

Mexico said nothing. "Okay," I said. "Definitely."

Señora touched Mexico's shoulder. Mexico looked at her and nodded. They said goodbye and walked off.

I sipped my iced tea. Mexico wrapped the rest of her carrots in her brown bag and gulped her water. I finished off the fries from my French bread pizza combo.

"Mr. Harrington and Señora did not mention this," I said. "But as your English Buddy, I think you should know that I get the stomach flu all the time. It's disgusting."

She kept drinking.

"I throw up easily," I whispered. "It's gross."

This big smile crept on to her face.

"Um, Mexico," I said, "is your aunt . . . friends with Hannah's mom?"

She shook her head. "My aunt is a . . ." She looked at the ceiling. "A housekeeper," she said firmly, "for the Andersons."

"Oh," I said. Mexico grinned. I let out a big breath. She and Hannah were not becoming friends.

The Conquistadores

A saguaro cactus can live to be two hundred years old. One night, when it's fifty or sixty (a teenager), white flowers grow out of its thick skin. But the very next day, the flowers curl into themselves. That's the only night, ever, that our state flowers grow. Good thing cacti are not extinct. Then there'd be no flowers.

Mexico and I finished our review of "The *Conquistadores*" for social studies. I'd read my *Suffragette Star* article about Art Attack aloud to her. I showed off the photos of Nathan and me, both wearing white underwear only, standing in muddy water up to our knees. We both have dirt smudged on our cheeks. My two baby front teeth are perfect, tiny flecks of white.

It was Sunday afternoon, and I, Lylice Martin, had a friend over. We were sitting together on my canopy bed. I hoped she didn't think it was babyish. Words tumbled out of my mouth like cereal into a bowl, *ping-ping-ping*ing into Mexico's ears.

"Oh, I love playing French horn. Even though it's hard. Like, you never know if a B flat is going to come out when you *mean* to play a B flat. Sometimes when I press the first valve down, an F comes out instead. But . . . I love band. It's like you're a piece of a big picture. And the picture can't exist without all the pieces." Mexico nodded. I swallowed and waited for her to say something. "How long have you played tuba?"

She looked up at my canopy and smiled. "Not too long. For just three weeks. Since school started," she said. Meatball leaped onto the bed and sniffed Mexico's skirt.

"I guess I wanted to play tuba because . . . maybe no one thought I could do it. Everybody look at you and think one thing, but really it's not the right thing."

"Yes," I said. "People always think the wrong

things about me too. Like that I'm trying to be perfect. Or that I'm too loud or that I can't stop talking or that I can't listen." I sighed. Mexico was the best person to talk to. She nodded as she scratched Meatball's tummy.

"I also picked tuba because no one else plays it. Ms. McGriff needed one," she said.

"Me too. That's why I chose French horn. We both picked a lonely brass instrument!" I had sprung to my feet without noticing, and I sat right back down on the bed. Mexico smiled and glanced at my window. "Oh! You can see Nathan's yard from here," I said. I got onto my knees, slid my curtains open, and muscled open my window. "See?"

We knelt and stared at the huge swimming pool. They even had a slide. Nathan Shelby's dad was a science fiction writer. His books were about meteors and one-eyed monsters and interplanetary wars. I read the two thin ones over the summer, after I'd finished the books on Mrs. Lanza's blue-ribbon reading list.

Nathan's real mom left when I was in kindergarten. Right after that, his first stepmom moved in, like she was waiting in the wings or something. A year later, after decorating the house with fake plants, she left. Nathan's second stepmom put weird sculptures in the backyard before she moved out. And stepmom three put in the pool and bought the trampoline and picnic tables. After Mr. Shelby got divorced from number three, his books started coming out.

"And there's Bear Mountain!" I said. "See?" Mexico leaned in close to me.

"Your favorite place," she said.

"Yes! We should go sometime," I said. "I mean, if you want."

"Yes, I do," she said. I felt like I would explode. The magic elevator from fourth grade to sixth was turning out to be the best ride I'd ever taken. We sat back down on my bed. Meatball pawed at a pillow, and then curled onto it, purring. Mexico patted down the hair over her ear.

"Mexico," I said. "Um . . ."

"Yes?" she said.

"Well . . . why do you always cover your one ear like that?"

She looked down at Meatball, who jumped off the bed and pattered over to her scratching post. My heart thunked. What if she didn't want to talk about it? What if it was none of my business?

"I mean, I don't need to know. I love ears. I love them. I do. I love to talk to them, and to . . . hear with them . . ."

Mexico giggled, and her nose wrinkled. She gingerly spread her fingers wide. Her nails were painted a beautiful dark red. She took a deep breath. Her hand sailed up to the hair on her right side. She lifted it up. Turned her ear to me. Something that looked like a folded brown leaf sat where an ear should be. It was an ear that curled into itself.

"Oh," I whispered.

There really wasn't anything else to say. I guessed she could hear out of the left ear but not the right. I didn't need to know if she was born that way. It seemed like a lot of things had happened to Mexico, by the way she never talked about any of them.

Right then a hot, sour smell came, along with the small sound of liquid pouring into something tin.

"Meatball, no!"

My cheeks burned as I rushed to swat her wet nose. I told Mexico how Meatball had used my air

41

vent as a litter box ever since I got her, and no matter how many times I told her no, she kept it up. My face felt hotter than a pepper, but I didn't care because Mexico was over.

"Girls! Soup's on!" my dad called.

"Coming!" I yelled. I waited for Mexico while she took her insulin in the bathroom, and then we headed into the kitchen.

There was a big salad, wheat rolls, brown rice stir-fry, and glasses of sugar-free lemonade. It was all stuff that Mexico could eat. And she ate. For someone who was so small, and who was only allowed to eat certain things, Mexico ate more than a truck driver. The meal was delicious. My mom winked at me.

I knew she'd left the veterinarian's office early to cook dinner for us, which was rare. Our refrigerator was always full of vegetables and meats that I knew my mom planned to use in recipes, but because of her schedule everything usually went rotten. She was a receptionist. But she was also taking two night classes to finish her bachelor's degree.

"Dad, how can Harrington just cut art?" I asked as I munched on a roll.

"Well, Lily-bean, he's trying to spend taxpayers' money in a way that'll let him keep his job."

"Huh?" I asked. "Taxpayers were paying for Art Attack?"

"Mitch, let's tone it down tonight," said my mom. "We have a guest," she added, smiling at Mexico, who smiled back.

"It's okay," my dad said. "Lylice has questions. Bean, taxpayers pay for public schools. And they pay Harrington's salary. Sad thing is," he said, ladling more rice onto his plate, "he's probably getting pressure from the higher-ups to use the budget for academics, not art. And Harrington wants to keep his job. There comes a time—"

"Mitchell, please."

"Come on, Sharon! This is important stuff, right, Lil?"

"Yes! Mom, just give us a second," I said. I hoped Mexico didn't think we were weird. "Finish, Dad."

"There comes a time where you have to decide what's more important: the humanities or a paycheck," he said.

"But art's as important as academics!" I said.

"Bean, you do still have band, right?" he asked, winking at Mexico. "Maybe you should just let it be—"

"Dad," I whined, "band is not the point! Not everyone's *in* band. But *everyone* did art. It was a way for the whole school to do something fun together. And now we don't have that. I think what Harrington did is completely repungant!"

My dad glanced at my mom, who bit her lip.

"*Repugnant,* Lily-bean. *Re-pug-nant,*" he said.

"Whatever!" I slammed my fist on the table. "You know what I mean. What he did completely stinks!"

"Lylice, that's enough. Come on. Guys, let's have dinner be *dinner* tonight," my mom said.

"How ya doin' there, Mexico?" asked my dad.

"Fine, thank you," she said.

"But, Dad, what if there's funny business going on here?" I asked.

"Lil," he said, sipping his lemonade, "just because Principal Harrington's not as creative as you'd like—"

"Oh, he's beyond not creative, Dad. We have no debating group at our school, no drama club. Now,

44

no arts and crafts. I mean, a piece of moldy bread has more imagination than he does. A dead cactus does!"

"Guys, enough," my mom said, pointing her fork at my dad. "You can do point-counterpoint another night." She turned to Mexico and smiled.

"So, Lylice has told us all about you," she said. Mexico's dimples came out slowly.

"What a great name: Mexico Mendoza!" my dad said with a big grin. He had the same teeth I did, and he didn't seem to care. Someday I wouldn't either, I hoped. "We should start the Double M club: Mexico Mendoza, Mitch Martin. Cool!" Mexico smiled and nodded.

"So is your family still in Nogales?" my mom asked.

Mexico nodded. "Some of them," she said.

"Can you imagine, Mom? Coming to live in another country? To a new school? By yourself? Where you don't know anybody?" It made my move from fourth to sixth seem like a baby step.

"What a big move, Mexico. Incredible," my dad said, shaking his head. "You're welcome over here at our house any time." He helped himself to another roll.

"You are a brave girl," my mom said.

Mexico stared at her plate. I stared at her. It was true. I'd never met anyone as brave as her. I almost could not stand the pride I felt that she was my friend.

"Mexico came here to get a better education and better medicine for her diabetes, but it turns out her aunt's not making much more here as Hannah Anderson's maid than her dad does as a taxi driver in Nogales," I said. This all fell out of my mouth the way you might try to pour someone one Tangy Tart but end up pouring them ten.

"I'm sorry . . ." I said.

Mexico's face and neck were blotchy. No one said anything. I'd ruined dinner.

"Damn it!" I said, slamming my fork onto the table. I cupped my hand over my mouth. No one even chewed.

"Lylice Martin," my dad warned. "Watch your mouth, young lady." "Young lady" was not what you wanted to be called when you had a friend over for the first time.

46

"Sorry. Sorry, Mexico," I said.

I swallowed a huge gulp of lemonade. Too quickly. My stomach gurgled. Mexico glanced down at it. My tummy squished and warbled so loud that you could almost see the digestive process happening inside of me. Mexico started giggling. She was so full of dimples that the whole table laughed with her.

"Double M, we heard you got an A on your essay. Congratulations," my dad said. "That is really cool."

"Thank you. I have a good teacher," said Mexico. "A good Buddy," she added. My parents laughed. Mexico patted her hair over her ear. Was it wrong to feel good about the ear right then? I was certainly not glad she had it, but she had shared her secret with me. I would never tell a soul.

"And your artwork is stunning," said my mom, pointing to Mexico's painting of the bus, which was hanging on the fridge. Mexico's cheeks grew red and she peeked at me out of the corner of her eye.

"We're so glad that you've become such a good friend to Lylice," my mom said. Was my mom about to cry? Uh-oh. I glanced at her with a watch-it look. *Please, please don't tell her that no one ever comes over here.* She didn't. If I had had thicker hair and

47

normal teeth, I might have come out beautiful like my mom.

"We're awfully glad to finally meet you, M.M.," my dad said, winking at Mexico.

"Thank you," she said.

"Mom," I said, standing up. "Can we help with dishes?" I noticed that Mexico had cleaned her plate.

"No, you girls go finish your dioramas."

"Yup, go ahead. We'll call you for dessert. Ske-daddle!" My dad grinned and blotted his chin with his napkin.

My mom and dad cleaned up after dinner, even though they had worked all day and had to wake up early tomorrow. Mexico and I went back into my room with mugs of sugar-free hot chocolate and started gluing diorama stuff together. Hers was on *Old Yeller* and mine was on *Of Mice and Men*.

Mrs. Lanza had said it didn't matter what book you chose, just that you'd actually read it and were creative. Creative! Ha! Thank goodness Susan B. Anthony Middle School teachers were good enough to make up for a shoddy administration.

Before dessert, Mexico went into the bathroom

to check her blood sugar. She took her backpack in with her.

"Mexico!" I called down the hall after five minutes. "You okay?"

"Yes," she said. "Okay."

"Dessert's coming soon!" I yelled. She came back just as my dad peeked in carrying two bowls of the juiciest strawberries and cream in North America.

"Enjoy, ladies," he said. I smelled potato chips on his breath. He ducked out, closing the door behind him.

"Is your B.S. all right?" I asked.

"Ninety-six," she said.

B.S. was our code for *blood sugar.* I explained to Mexico what *B.S.* usually stood for in English. We thought it was fun to say the abbreviation for bad words but not *mean* the bad words. I'd never been with Mexico when the B.S. was anything other than ninety-six or a hundred or something normal like that. Mr. Harrington was right. Diabetes was very manageable.

"Mexico, your diorama is exquisite!" I said through spoonfuls of whipped cream.

Old Yeller had his face in his yellow water bowl,

and the old farmer leaned against a red barn and held a tiny shotgun. You could see in his eyes that he felt torn.

"You are so good. You really are," I said. Mexico grinned and stared into her strawberries, chewing. Meatball sat in her lap, sniffing the bowl.

In my diorama, Lennie stood in his bunk, alone. Unfortunately, the cotton bunnies surrounding him ended up just looking like snow.

"Um, I'm . . . I'm sorry if I told my parents all about—"

"It's okay."

I didn't want her to leave.

"I mean, I only wanted them to know that you are just so . . . cool." My dad's word. What an understatement.

Mexico patted her hair over her ear. "So are you," she said.

I felt like someone had just put a crown on my head. Mexico Mendoza, the best-dressed, prettiest, funnest girl I ever met thought I was cool. I climbed onto my bed, and we sat cross-legged, with Meatball in between us.

"Mexico, you are going to be a famous painter when you grow up."

"Hmm," she said, looking up into my canopy. She shrugged. "Maybe. I love to paint."

"You're a natural," I said. She smiled.

"And you," she said. "Maybe you will be a writer. For the . . . newspaper. A big newspaper."

"Yes," I said. "I love writing about current events!" We discussed the state of affairs at Susan B. Anthony Middle School. Art Attack, we both agreed, was an issue that needed attention. It wasn't fair that the taxpayer money was not being stretched to cover the costs of art when lots of kids were good at it, like Mexico.

We decided we'd create a blog; a very special blog for the lost and downtrodden students of Susan B. Anthony. I brought my dad's laptop into my room, and we got online and got down to business. It turned out to be easy. All you had to do was answer some questions, and you had your very own blog. We decided to call it the Nogales Flowers Arts Initiative. It sounded really official, and when you go online, you have to do that if you want to be taken seriously. In

51

our profile, we said that arts and crafts helped kids be confident through school.

Our first post was called "The Death of the Humanities" and it was a petition to bring back Art Attack. If we got enough signatures, maybe Harrington would reconsider. If he was the boss of that tax money, shouldn't he decide how it was spent?

"Leelas, *somos conquistadores*!" She held up her frayed copy of *Living in Our World,* our social studies text.

"*Si,* Mexico! *Nosotros somos* sixth-grade *conquistadores!*"

She clapped.

"But . . ." I shook my finger. "Remember that the *real* conquistadors were European savages who wanted blood, goods, and land." Then I reconsidered. "You're right. They *were* conquerors. And we shall *conquer* the administration with our blog!"

She held her hand up and I slapped her a five. I wished she could stay forever. We checked the blog again, and Gorpat Geetha had signed the petition!

At 7:30 p.m., Mexico's aunt beeped from the truck. I walked Mexico outside. She climbed into the front seat with her diorama and backpack. My parents waved from our porch.

"Bye. Thanks for coming over," I said, smiling at her aunt, who waved.

"Bye, Leelas. Thank you," Mexico said, grinning. Her nose wrinkled.

"Hasta mañana!" I called as the truck turned around and headed back down Saguaro Circle.

I stood still, staring after them and then into the sky. The Sunday sun had sunk behind Bear Mountain. Tucson stars were gigantic, like celestial tennis balls. There was something neat in the silence right then, kind of like the way music lingered a second after Ms. McGriff had cut off the band.

THE SUFFRAGETTE STAR

VOLUME 2

ARTIAC ARREST
by Lylice Martin, Staff Writer

An artiac arrest occurs when the supply of creative blood to the heart is reduced or stopped. If the supply is shut down for a long time, the heart becomes lazy, dull, monotonous, repetitive, tedious, and BORING.

Beep. Beep. Beep. Beep . . .

. . . goes the artbeat monitor machine.
The artbeat of the Susan B. Anthony arts program slowly begins its painful journey toward heaven. Or reincarnation.

Beeeeep. Beeeeep. Beeeeep. Beeeeep.

The pulse slows down. Even. More.

To prevent an artiac arrest:
• Exercise your right to freedom of speech and tell your school faculty that you disapprove.
• Cut back on fatty activities, such as watching television and running up high

cell phone bills, and get off your duff and take a stand.

• Ask your principal for healthy options to the program, rather than cutting it altogether.

Beeeeeeep. Beeeeeeep. Beeeeeeep.

With heavy arts, we say farewell to our beloved program. Did our innocent program see this coming? Does life ever really know when death is near? And what about all of those buried, creative ideas in students' minds? Will they ever live to see the light of day?

Beeeeeeeeeeeeeeeeeeeeeeeeeeeeeeee eeeeeeeeeeeeeeeeeeeeeeeeeeeeee eeeeeeeeeeeeeeeeeeeeeeeeeep.

The decision to cut Art Attack is not a popular one. I urge you to voice your opinions to those who have the power, in hopes of reviving our construction paper, glitter, pastels, watercolors, clay, and googly eyes. But most important, to resurrect our own potential to become great creators and thinkers.

Log on to:
http://nogalesflowers.blogspot.com
to sign the petition!

The Newspaper Biz

After Mr. Shelby dropped Nathan and me off, I rushed up to the supply office in Ballot Hall. I knew Mrs. Lanza would be making copies of the *Suffragette Star*. I had seen my second article all formatted on her computer screen, but I couldn't wait to see it in print.

"Hi, Mrs. . . . ! Oh," I said. Principal Harrington turned around. "Hello, Principal Harrington. I was expecting to see Mrs. Lanza. Is the paper ready?" I asked.

"Not quite yet, Lylice. Today the paper will come out after school instead of before. Get on to class."

"Oh," I said. "Why?"

"Now, just . . . I've had to make a few . . . changes," he said.

"Changes?" I asked.

"Yes."

We stared at each other. Harrington pulled a tissue from the bottom of his jacket sleeve and dabbed his forehead. Then he straightened his green bow tie.

"But Mrs. Lanza's the newspaper adviser," I said.

"Lylice. I just saw fit to make a few changes. Now get on to class."

"All right," I said. A heavy feeling followed me all day. Whenever I saw Harrington, I felt as if we had come upon each other crossing a bridge from opposite sides. We always seemed to be blocking each other in some way. I couldn't concentrate in any classes. What changes? Whose articles did he change? And why? I drove Mexico crazy.

During band, Harrington came on the PA system. Through gritted teeth, Miss McGriff told us to put our instruments down.

"Greetings, students. The *Suffragette Star* will be available right after school in the gym. Pick up your copy and show your Trailblazer pride. Thank you."

Right after band I headed straight to the gym.

Mexico told me to hurry up and go and not bother to wait for her. She knew I was going nuts.

If you got the newspaper, you got five extra-credit points from Mrs. Lanza, so lots of kids got it. Mrs. Lanza handed out the papers, and you had to sign your name on a sheet when you took one. I stood in the gym with my brain-on-wheels and flipped through the paper.

What? Wait . . . I flipped through again. I didn't see my article anywhere. Wait a minute. There it was.

A teaser?

Harrington had edited my feature down to a *teaser?* A feature was a page or a half a page. A teaser was one eighth of the page or smaller. Instead of my whole Art Attack article, on the last page of the paper at the bottom right corner it said:

> With heavy arts, we say farewell to our beloved
> arts program.—**Lylice Martin, Staff Writer**

What? It didn't even make sense. Wasn't that censorship? Weren't there laws in sixth grade? Preposterous. Double preposterous.

"Mrs. Lanza," I said. "Did you see what happened to my article?"

"Yes, sweet girl," she said, handing Sari Henderson and two girls their papers.

"Principal Harrington *edited* it out," I said.

She sighed and shook her head. "Ms. Martin . . . it's the breaks of the biz. Just think," she said, throwing her purple scarf over her shoulder, "when you're a bigtime journalist, *you'll* get to edit people's articles."

I marched straight to Harrington's office, ready for a fight. He wasn't in. My heart tightened. Kids were trampling past me and out of Ballot Hall. I didn't see Mexico. I wished I'd waited for her after band.

It wasn't fair. I dragged my brain-on-wheels down the Ballot Hall steps. I noticed that both garbage bins on the Great Lawn were loaded with *Suffragette Stars*. Nobody cares about what's in them, they just want their five crummy points. I trudged down the rest of the steps.

Almost at the bottom, I spotted him. The beast. Aha!

"Excuse me, Principal Harrington. I just picked up my *Suffragette Star.*"

"Good, Lylice. You'll get your extra five from Mrs. Lanza," he said, trotting up the steps.

"Yes. But . . ." I stopped talking, and he kept going, right past me. Was it wrong to confront him? I swallowed hard. "But you cut my article, Principal Harrington. Why . . . ?" It was out. I had done it. He stopped.

"Lylice, now, please, first of all *Mr.* Harrington is fine. And I just . . . I . . . we were over on word count," he said, then continued up the steps.

"But . . ." My brain-on-wheels and I followed him up. I had come this far. "But nobody told me about word count! Isn't that censorship?"

Harrington stood for a second with his back to me. His head was down. He let out a breath, then skittered up the steps and disappeared into Ballot Hall. I stood in the middle of the steps, speechless. Kids whizzed by me, heading down. Very slowly, I dragged my brain-on-wheels to the Great Lawn.

Tap tap tap.

"Come on, Leelas. I see your dad," said Mexico, who had come up next to me. We walked to the curb.

"Mexico," I said. "Principal Harrington hates me."

"No he does not," she said.

"He changed . . . ," I said. It seemed silly to talk about the article anymore. What was done was done.

"I know. Mrs. Lanza told me. Do you want to know what else she told me?" she asked. I nodded. "That she told him to keep his nose *out* of the newspaper business from now on."

Destruir

Spanish Vocab:

- *beber:* to drink
- *sentar:* to sit
- *saltar:* to jump
- *tocar:* to play
- *levantar:* to stand up
- *preguntar:* to ask
- *que hora es:* What time is it?
- *bailar:* to dance
- *leer:* to read
- *bienvenidos:* Welcome
- *comer:* to eat
- *exclamar:* to shout
- *aplaudir:* to clap

- *torcer:* to bend
- *caminar:* to come; to walk
- *destruir:* to destroy
- *qué pasa:* What's happening?
- *muy malo:* very bad

The Spanish project: Pick three verbs from the vocabulary list. Don't tell what they are. Act them out. Whoever in class guesses the most verbs, in Spanish, wins a prize.

Señora Schwartz wore Juicy Jeans (I'm pretty sure they were genuine), a purple blouse, pink sandals, and bright makeup. Her room looked like Cinco de Mayo happened 365 days a year.

Tony Frizell (Paco *en español*) was first. He *beber*ed a soda. He *comer*ed Cheese Chomps. And then he *saltar*ed up and down. We all yelled out his verbs at the same time. Señora gave him a squeeze and pinched his beet red cheek.

Hannah Anderson (Juanita) *tocar*ed the harmonica (poorly), *levantar*ed from her chair, and *preguntar*ed Señora a question *("¿Que hora es?")*. Everyone called out each of Hannah's verbs. Señora hugged her.

Nathan Shelby (Pedro) actually *bailar*ed, then *comer*ed a banana, and *leer*ed a line from *Bienvenidos,* our Spanish text. Everyone laughed. It was a great presentation.

"Boooo," yelled Mike Black.

"Miguel, mi amigo, boo you. *Parate,"* Señora said. *"¡Excelente, Presidente* Shelby, *mi amigo!"* She *bailar*ed as she *exclamar*ed, and *aplaudir*ed while *torcer*ing her hips. She hugged Nathan, who was blushing. I thought I saw him give Hannah a shy look as he threw away half the banana, but then I didn't think so. But did he? I squished down my feelings for later.

"¡Concepción!" Señora called, nodding at me. *"Ven camina!"*

I bolted to the front of the room and stood next to Señora's Frida Kahlo poster.

Silence.

I dug my two front teeth into my lower lip. My face felt hot. Barrettes dangling. Hands shaking. I wiped my palms onto my flowered jeans. Everyone's eyes studied me.

There is that second in time where you decide to turn back. Where you say, *Well, I thought it was a good idea, but now that I'm doing it, it's not so good. Time to shove it.* But I didn't shove it. I swallowed and looked at Señora. Her smile had turned stiff, into an I'm-not-sure-if-I'm-going-to-like-this smile. Before I chickened out, I threw myself at the Frida Kahlo, ripped it down with both hands, and then tore it in half.

Chaos!

"¡Concepción!" Señora yelled.

The entire room gasped. Everyone's eyes were huge. Paco shouted, "Bone!" Pedro's mouth hung open. Juanita stared at Señora. Miguel pounded his desk and laughed. Mexico nodded.

"Lylice, *qué pasa?*" Señora yelled. I'd ripped right through Frida's face.

"¿Destruir?" I said. *"Destruir* is my first verb . . . ?"

No one had guessed it. I was sent to the office. With no hug.

"Bring back art, don't destroy it! *No destruyas!*" I shouted as I left the room. Two minutes later I faced Harrington and his breakfast sandwich.

"Detention? But I didn't do anything!" I cried.

It was over. Everything. High school. College.

Business school. Law school. Veterinary school. Yale School of Drama. All of them were out of the question. I'd never, ever had detention. Ever. This was it. I imagined Harrington enthusiastically waving me down the steps of Ballot Hall; Mrs. Garrison frowning as I arrived at Catalina Elementary; kids glaring at me as I enter their fifth-grade classroom, one throwing an egg that splats in my face.

"Now, Lylice, you can't tell me that you've done nothing wrong," he said. "Surely you're bright enough to know that."

"I am bright. That's why I picked verbs like *destruir*, to destroy. Nobody guessed it."

"Well, Lylice, tearing up a school poster in the classroom is defacing school property."

"It wasn't a *school* poster. Señora probably bought it at the mall with her own money. Like I did." I unzipped my brain-on-wheels and produced the same Frida Kahlo poster. "I'm going to give it to her. I was only making a statement about art. And how we shouldn't destroy it." It had seemed like a good idea at home.

"Lylice, lower your voice."

"I'm sorry. Anyway, this was an assignment. You're giving me detention because I did the assignment? This school is not fair." I didn't know how far I could push it, but I supposed I'd find out.

"Now, Lylice, what is fair is taking responsibility for what you've done wrong."

"Doing homework is wrong?"

"Lylice, now, enough. This conversation is over. I'll see you Friday afternoon when the final bell rings. You can report to me."

"But I have tennis on Wednesdays and Fridays. I can't—"

His mouth had frozen open around his sandwich. Instead of biting, he said: "Make time, Lylice. Goodbye."

What a rat.

That night, with Meatball purring next to me, I calculated my GPA. Señora had given me a C on the *vocabulario* project, and because of that, I was somewhere in the neighborhood of a 2.5. Horrible. So far, my first-quarter grades were *muy malo*. I was definitely not meeting standards.

If I were a cat, I wouldn't care about meeting

standards. I would care about licking sour cream off a spoon, lying on the bathroom rug in front of the heater, or chasing a cricket. She might be just a cat, but Meatball knew things. Things you couldn't know if you were a person who thinks too hard. Like me.

I have started to question my potential.

The Green Card Fiasco

"Mmmm . . . *delicioso*. I love green chilies," I said. "The spicier, the better!" Mexico nodded. We sat at lunch, sharing cold quesadillas left over from the Mendozas' dinner last night.

As Tony and Nathan passed our table, I heard Tony say his mother would be out of town for the whole weekend. He and Nathan high-fived.

"Hey, Walrus!" said Tony, walking over to us. Nathan elbowed Tony. He waved at Mexico and me, and kept walking. I saw him sit down at the yellow table with Debbie.

"Hey yourself, Tony," I said.

"How's your little beaner girlfriend, Lie-lice? Are you going to marry her so she can get her green card?"

Tony said, smooching the air. Mexico stared down at her lunch. I could barely speak.

"*Don't* pick on Mexico," I said, bolting off the bench and facing Tony. I could handle him. I wasn't scared.

"Lylice, chill!" he said, giggling and taking a step back.

"I don't *feel* like chilling!" I yelled.

"What, Lie-*lice?* It's not—it's not a big deal," said Tony. "My dad talks about Mexicans all the time. So shut your flipping mouth!" He flicked at the air in front of me with his thumb and middle finger.

"And how is your dad, Tony? Still in jail?"

Color vanished from his face.

"Shut up, Lylice," said Tony through clenched teeth.

"Is he? Huh? Isn't that fun? Do you like it when someone at school talks about *your* personal stuff? *Do you?*"

"Lylice Martin, shut up." Tony's jaw jutted forward.

"Leave Mexico alone."

Just then Mike Black, carrying a heaping plate of

curly fries, lumbered in between us. He looked from me to Tony.

"What's the problem here?" he asked.

"None-ya," said Tony, gritting his teeth and staring up into Mike's eyes.

"What?" asked Mike, looking down at Tony.

"None-ya," snapped Tony. Instead of asking him once more what he meant, Mike just took a step closer.

"None-ya business!" Tony said, his lip quivering.

"If I decide to *make* it my business, Frizell," said Mike, "you're done." His eyes narrowed as he headed to his table, his ponytail swinging behind. Tony wiped his nose on the back of his hand. My eyes bored into his. Slowly, he backed away.

"Mexico, are you all right?" I asked, sitting down next to her.

"Yes, Leelas. But you shouldn't . . ."

Mexico didn't finish. She shook her head, and put her half-eaten quesadilla into her lunch sack. Lunch was ruined.

"He was out of line!" I said.

"But," Mexico said, smoothing the hair beside

71

her ear and looking from one of my eyes to the other, "you can just ignore someone like that." When Mexico looked at you, she looked at all of you, and she didn't let you get away with anything. I sighed. She was right.

Last year, when Tony was in fifth grade, Mr. Frizell was arrested for stealing money from people's bank accounts. The whole school knew about it. The year before, the rumor was that he had gotten caught stealing cars. For as long as I'd known Tony, his father had been doing bad things.

As we cleared our table, I glanced at the yellow table. Hannah was absent. Debbie and Nathan were talking. Nathan had walked away from Tony before the whole incident. Why did he need to be a part of the yellow table anyway?

Tony sat alone. When he wasn't furiously shoveling curly fries into his mouth, he was wiping his nose on the back of his hand. He had never said anything *that* mean to me. Nothing that I couldn't handle. And now I'd made him sad.

It wasn't *green card* that had irked me so much. Although it did make me wonder how a person from

Mexico got to be an American citizen, and whether or not Mexico was one. But how did you ask someone something like that?

What bothered me most was that Tony used the word *beaner* for a Mexican person. I wondered what else his father said about Mexican people. Tony kept wiping his eyes and nose while he gulped his lunch down in a frenzy.

I looked forward to going to tennis after school. Slamming that ball (when I actually hit it) always made me feel better. After lunch, I headed to math, and Mexico headed to the bathroom. Good thing Mr. Schvitter was at his desk eating salad. I parked my brain-on-wheels and took my seat.

"It was so out of line! And no teachers did anything, Mr. S. The only time they get involved is if someone is crying, or hurt."

"Lylice, you're right. It *was* out of line," said Mr. S., shaking his head and munching on a tomato. "Bottom line is, we need more chaperones during lunch. It's just plain silly to have only two." He licked his fingers. "Between you and me," he continued, wiping dressing off his chin with a checkered napkin, "I

73

think teachers know that you can handle things on your own, so they don't interfere. You're different, Lylice," he said. "Not like the typical riffraff hanging around these halls. You're above all that."

He winked at me, and then brushed crumbs off his lavender button-down shirt. I liked the sound of that. Being "above all that." I liked that wink, and Mr. S.'s way of acting like he wasn't telling anyone else what he was telling me.

"Thanks, Mr. S.," I said. "But when you're 'above it,' that means you aren't *in* it and you get . . . I don't know . . ." I leaned my cheek on my palm.

"Lylice, off the record, you don't want to be 'in it' with some of these kids."

I wished I could fully agree. At parent-teacher conferences last year, Mrs. Garrison told my parents that I had good instincts. Maybe it was the goodness of those instincts that told me Mr. S. was right. But the badness part of the instincts made me *want* to be in it with these kids.

Mr. S. ate his last crouton. Kids started filing in. Book bags were unzipped, math texts were slapped onto desks, people hollered and dropped into seats.

Mr. S. winked at me again. I didn't feel like smiling at him, but I did anyway. I felt nauseated.

By the time school was over, my stomach was making all kinds of growling noises, but I went to tennis anyway. We had to have it in the gym because there were no tennis courts. Coach Zito dragged out the saggy net and started setting it up. By the time he finished, his white oxford shirt was soaked because the gym wasn't air-conditioned.

Tony glared at me when we took the court for our volley. Great. Of all the partners to get today.

I swallowed hard. Was that salsa that I tasted? And green chilies? I gave Tony a weak smile. He looked away. Tony always won. I was glad I was about to be beaten. He deserved it after what I'd said to him.

Smack! Tony served a nice steady one out.

Bounce. *Thwack!* Wow. I returned it.

Tony was on a roll. I was too. My face was getting hot and my barrettes were coming loose. But I was really playing tennis. *We* were playing *together.* I was so excited I forgot about my gurgly stomach. And what I'd said to Tony was okay. He'd been rude.

There was that tummy gurgle again. I swallowed.

Salsa. Uh-oh. Wait. Wait. I took a deep breath. A horrible chili taste burned my throat when I swallowed. It felt like everything in my stomach was turning upside down and then right side up again.

Oh please, no. I swallowed again, *hard,* telling my lunch to stay put. Tony was hitting every shot, as usual, but today I was too. Kids were cheering. I didn't know for whom, but I pretended me. I was actually volleying!

Bounce. *Pang!* Another square-in-the-middle from Tony.

Bounce. *Blang!* I returned it. Again!

Bounce. Bounce. Bounce went the ball. Roll . . . Tony missed.

"Bone!" he shouted, throwing his racket onto the gym floor. I won the set! Uh-oh. Oh no. Oh please, no.

"Way to go, Lylice!" Coach Zito ran out onto the court, blowing his whistle. "Frizell, come shake hands with your partner," he ordered. Tony stamped over. He shot his hand out, over the floppy net. I grabbed my stomach. Oh yuck. Oh yuck yuck yuck . . .

"Congratulations, Walrus—"

Bleck blaaaaaaaeeeeeck . . . Salsacheesechicken-tortillachilies . . . I lifted my hand to my mouth but I couldn't stop it. I barfed all over Tony Frizell and the net.

"*Eeeeeeeck!*" Tony screamed. He jumped up and down. "Lylice, you jerk!"

"Whoa-ho!" said Coach. "Oh boy, oh boy. Lylice, to the ladies' room. Somebody," he called, "come walk Lylice to the bathroom, please. Frizell, be a man. Just go wash up right away." Kids screeched and held their noses. "Relax, people," said Coach.

"Jerk!" Tony said, still hopping around. It dripped from his arm, and it had splattered onto his white T-shirt. Hot tears poured down my cheeks. I kept swallowing and swallowing, trying to make the burning feeling go away.

"It's okay," Coach said, patting my back. Sari Henderson came to walk me to the girls' bathroom. "Sports fans," Coach was yelling as Sari and I walked off, "let's behave like ladies and gentlemen . . . *Relax!*"

Oh please, oh *please* let me make it. Sari watched me clap both hands to my mouth. We had to walk all the way to the other side of Ballot Hall to the girls' bathroom. Lucky boys. Their bathroom was right across from the entrance to the gym. Right when we got in, Sari guided me to a stall and opened it.

"Kneel down," she said, closing the stall door behind me. I knelt on the hard floor in front of the toilet. I threw up again. My throat felt like it had been lit on fire. Hair fell in my face and goo ran out of my nose. When I was through, I walked out, and Sari handed me a wad of toilet paper.

"Blow," she said. I blew.

"Rinse," she said, turning on a faucet. Taking in huge slurps of cold water felt good. Through watery eyes, I glanced at Sari in the mirror. She pulled her hair into a tighter bun. Her blue shorts matched the dolphin in the middle of her white tank top.

"Th-thanks . . ." I said. Sari shrugged.

"No biggie," she said. "I've got four little brothers that I look after. It's part of life." I splashed water on my face, wiped my nose, and redid my barrettes.

"Good going, by the way, beating Tony," she said, crossing her arms and leaning against a sink. "Now he knows he can't win *everybody*." Sari smiled. "Feel better?" she asked. I nodded.

But my head pounded. My shorts were stained. It stung when I swallowed. And worst of all, Tony was going to hate me even more than he already did.

I followed her out of the bathroom. Kids were filing out of the gym. They fanned the air and made squinty faces at me. Sari grabbed her backpack, and in a flash, she was gone with the rest of the tennis team. Coach was dunking the net into a sudsy bucket. He jogged over and patted me on the back.

"You okay, kid?" he asked. I nodded. "Impressive job today, anyway. Good for you," he said. I tried to smile but didn't open my mouth for fear something besides words would pour out. I dragged my brain-on-wheels out of the gym and into Ballot Hall.

The boys' bathroom door burst open and there stood a dripping-wet Tony Frizell. He stared me down. His white T-shirt was drenched, so you could see his pink skin underneath it. Fat drops of water dribbled from his curly hair. It was as if he had taken a shower in the sink. He smelled like drainpipes and powdered soap. A long splotch of brown throw-up had stained the bottom of his shirt.

I opened my mouth to apologize, but nothing came out (thank goodness).

Dear Nathan,

I won a volley against Tony in tennis! I
still can't believe it. I don't think he can,
either. Are you going to the Halloween
Sock Hop? I am. Mexico and I are helping decorate the gym. I can't believe it's
in four weeks! I was thinking I would be a
crayon. Or a bookmark. Or a green chili.
Are you going?

W/B/S,

Lylice Martin

<u>A Limerick for You</u>
There was a band teacher who tried
To make her musicians abide.
One trombone was behaved.
The other made her enraged.
But Ms. McGriff said she'd just let it slide.

Mexico's Brilliant Idea

"Nate," said Mr. Shelby, "you're coming right home after school today. Math tutor's coming."

In the rearview mirror, I saw Nathan roll his eyes. Then he stared out his window.

"It's fine to do well in English, but you gotta be consistent. I don't get it, Nathan. Did you know that neither of your brothers needed tutors?"

Nathan shrugged, still staring out at cars passing by. Then he glanced into the mirror and, of course, I was looking at him. My cheeks immediately burned. He smiled. My heart pounded and my mouth felt dry. Before I knew it, I was imagining a pair of puckered lips popping out of the rearview mirror. Then a nose, and then those two blue eyes. I am pulled toward the mirror like a magnet. I kiss those lips. *What is wrong with me?*

"Believe it or not, Miss Lylice, this buffoon does have a brain. He *will* make honor roll this quarter. And, he'll ace his AIMS," he said. "Right, Nate?" Mr. Shelby glanced at his son out of the corner of his eye. "Right?" Nathan was watching the man in the next car flick a cigarette out his window. He still didn't answer.

Mr. Shelby's cell phone rang Beethoven's Fifth. He clicked on his earpiece. "This is Stuart Shelby." I wondered what Beethoven would think if he heard his enormous masterpiece peeping from a tiny piece of metal.

"Well, well, well, hello, Michelle," said Mr. Shelby. "Thank *you*. It was great to chat with you too." We pulled up to the curb in front of the Great Lawn and Mr. Shelby waved at us as we climbed out. "You know, I just don't think I can. I've actually been meaning to delete my profile . . . ," he was saying as I closed the back door.

Before English, I handed Nathan my note.

"Thanks," he said. "I kinda needed this today." A bubbling feeling twirled all the way from my feet to my lips, and I could not stop smiling.

"Oh, hey," he said. "I heard you beat Tony in tennis. Pretty sweet, Lylice. You are really tough." Nathan patted my back. I melted. If I'd known he was going to touch me, I would have worn something better than my fake Juicy Jeans and an orange sweater.

"Thanks, Nathan," I said.

"See ya," he said, joining Tony Frizell, who was strutting down the hall in baggy jeans and what looked like brand-new tennis shoes. Maybe his mom had bought him a new outfit. Good. Maybe he'd forgotten about the barf. And how much he hated me.

In English, Mrs. Lanza gave a poetry pop quiz. We had to identify haiku and limericks. Cinchy. I knew I got the extra credit for identifying the surprise sonnet at the bottom of the page too. So I definitely I got an A. I sure needed one. Poetry had been my favorite unit. After class, I approached Tony in the hall.

"Hey, Tony," I said. He kept walking. I rushed to keep up alongside him.

"I apologize for—"

"Don't. Get some braces, Walrus!" He screwed up his face into a mess and continued down the hall.

That was that. I took a big breath. Something in

me unlocked. I still wished I hadn't said what I'd said about his dad, but at least Tony Frizell was back to being Tony Frizell. Good thing, because Mexico and I had important work to do. At lunch, we discussed the petition on the Nogales Flowers Arts Initiative blog. After a week, we had only eighteen signatures. My parents were two.

"Even if we *did* get more signatures, who knows," I said, biting my lip. "It's Harrington's tax money to spend however he wants." Mexico munched on celery and peanut butter, and looked at the ceiling. We needed a new plan.

"What if . . ." Mexico stopped and thought. "What if the money doesn't come from the taxes?"

"Where does it come from?" I asked, taking a bite of rice from my burrito combo.

"Okay," said Mexico. "My aunt said Hannah Anderson has this big house and this pool and . . . so much," she whispered. "What if we ask some parents to give money? For we can start *after-school* art class?"

"Aha! Mexico, you're brilliant." I lowered my voice. "*Harrington* could send out letters. He could say art was canceled because of low funding and what a shame. Then say that if parents could afford it, they could mail a donation."

Mexico nodded.

"It's worth a try," I said.

"I think so. But, Leelas, how do we get Harrington to . . . ?"

"Well," I said, "if we could get him to write something . . ." It seemed like a very complicated idea. "Or we could write the letters ourselves, but he would have to sign them," I said. "It would have to look really official."

"But how . . . ?" she asked.

"I don't know," I said. "But we'll figure something out."

After school, Principal Harrington, who oozed breath mints and beans, gestured me into his office. I took a big breath.

For one hour, Cornelius Harrington III acted busy, fiddling with papers, books, and files. I was to fold my hands on the small desk across from his, sit quietly, and "think about what I did." Ha! Two things that I am terrible at: staying still and being quiet. For one full hour? Bone.

I couldn't help being jealous of the tennis team,

who were serving and volleying while I was being still. All the thoughts I had about "what I did" were long gone. My mind was on Miss Mendoza scrubbing Hannah Anderson's filthy floors. And on the petition. And most important, on Harrington.

His desk wasn't fancy; the peeling, wood-colored paint revealed a dirty-white desk underneath. The school definitely needed more money. For lots of things.

Harrington's black loafer tapped fast on the brown-orange carpet. The fringes on the top of his shoe shimmied with each tap. Minutes dragged.

"Excuse me, Principal Harrington," I blurted out, "if this time would benefit you more elsewhere, I, too, have a lot of other commitme—"

"Lylice, close it. This is punishment. Now, zip it."

I slouched. Nathan's shy face when he looked at Hannah after his *vocabulario* project popped into my head. I shoved the thought down for later.

Harrington talked softly into the phone about how many crullers he needed for the end-of-quarter dough-nut party. He growled under his breath that what he really needed was a "damn" secretary to help him arrange these events.

Seconds inched by.

He finished his phone call and then dialed another number. After giving directions to the school, he said he was looking forward to meeting the person at the interview next week. I sighed loudly. His head snapped up. He finished his call and hung up the phone.

"Principal Harrington?"

"Lylice, enough. You are to sit *quietly.*"

"I know, but can I just—"

"No you *can't.* This is a detention," he said.

"Yes, Principal Harrington." My heart was thumping so hard it almost burst out of my sweater.

"Lylice," he said, rubbing his forehead. "You don't have to call me *Principal* Harrington. *Mr.* will do just fine."

"Just a sign of respect," I said.

"I appreciate that."

I had to go for it. With all the courage I could find, I opened my mouth. "Um, Mr. Harrington, do you think I'm meeting standards?" I asked. He leaned back in his seat. Our eyes were stuck on each other's. There we were, at that bridge again. It felt so weird I looked at my hands. My whole face was hot.

"Lylice . . . ," he said. "Your grades aren't up to what Mrs. Garrison and I know you're capable of, but you're doing well. *Very* well, considering your age."

Magic words! "Thank you, Mr. Harrington," I said. He nodded and started marking on a piece of paper.

I was here to stay.

Here with Mexico and Nathan and Mrs. Lanza and the paper and tennis and Coach and Mr. Schvitter and band and everything. I pressed my lips together so I wouldn't smile so big. But I couldn't help it. And I could get my grades up. I knew I could.

Mr. Harrington liked me.

I got even braver.

"Can schools take donations from parents? To pay for things like Art Attack?" I asked.

Harrington's eyebrows met each other right above his nose. "Lylice," he said, rubbing his forehead. "I'll worry about those matters, you worry about schoolwork. And *that's it*. Now, zip it."

"But if we sent out letters to parents, asking—"

"Lylice, stop. Now, enough," he said. "*We're* not going to do anything of the sort. Parents have got their minds on more important things, like their children passing their AIMS in February."

"But maybe art was the only thing keeping some kids *in* school. Look how many days Mike Black has missed since the program was cut. Kids can't take AIMS if they're not present!"

"Lylice. This conversation is over."

"But—"

"Over," said Harrington. "You are here for detention. Not discussion. That's it." He lifted a stack of papers, straightened them, and slammed them back onto his desk. The top one floated to the floor. A sheet of Susan B. Anthony Middle School stationery.

THE SUFFRAGETTE STAR

VOLUME 3

THE AMERICAN INDIAN: FIRST COME, LAST SERVED

by Lylice Martin, Staff Writer

People are very proud of their homes. This roving reporter caught up with three students after school on the Great Lawn. Sixth-grader Tony Frizell, who lives in an apartment with his sister and mother, said: "My house is the best! I just got my own TV!"

Eighth-grade class president Sari Henderson's room is her favorite room in her house because "it's private." And Nathan Shelby, sixth-grade class president, claims his backyard is "the best place to hang out."

Imagine one night you are on the phone, surfing the Net, or hanging out in your room, and there is a knock at the front door. It's new people, who eat dinner at your house and tell your parents that they are going to give them money for the dinner. But then your parents ask you to pack up all of your stuff and tell you that you have to move because the people are moving into your house. And that's that.

"I bet people couldn't do that nowadays," Shelby commented.

But why, Mr. President? People get kicked out of their houses nowadays all the time because of money.

Sixth-grader Mike Black, a member of the Iroquois tribe, could not be reached for comment.

There is a lot of money that goes all over the place in the world. Some of it you can't even see. You just know it goes toward things like playgrounds and airplanes.

But the most money is spent on machine guns and the least money is spent on the people who found America. The next time you open the door to your home or close the door to your room, remember the knock on the door that forced an entire race of people out of their homes. Forever.

Log on to:

http://nogalesflowers.blogspot.com

to post your photos of home and to sign an *important petition!*

The Map Incident

The assignment: Pick a person from local history. State his or her goals and ambitions. How did that person contribute to our region?

The Hohokams were the very first people to live in Tucson, twelve thousand years ago, before the Anglo-Saxons came and kicked them off the land.

I dressed as Chief Hohokam. I was the only one who created a costume for the project. It wasn't even a question that I would wear a headdress and my hair in two braids.

As the honorable chief, I pleaded with my fellow sixth-graders: "Give me back my land! I have slept, cried, danced, and killed and ate the buffalo of this land! Give it back! Give it back!"

Hannah Anderson looked amused. Coach stared at me. Tony laughed. Nathan gave me a big smile. Mexico nodded.

"All righty, Lylice, thank you. Thank you. Nice costume," said Coach, clearing his throat. I was on fire.

"Coach, don't you think what we white people did was just preposterous?" I asked, lifting the floppy feathers out of my eyes.

"Well, Lylice, these things happen. Awful things, I agree. It's up to us to learn from these things and move on, and see to it that these things don't repeat themselves."

If he said *these things* one more time, I would scream. He was doing that thing that teachers do sometimes, where they say things that sound like they're coming right from a textbook.

"But *these things* do keep happening," I said. "It's not fair. Christopher Columbus wasn't some big hero! He killed the Native Americans too, just like the conquistadors!"

People were looking from Coach to me, and then back to Coach and then back to me. The room was buzzing and people were awake. Nathan nodded at me. My heart leaped out of my chest and danced on Coach's desk. Hannah and Debbie were listening to me. Tony raised his fists in the air. Mexico Mendoza sat up straight and her dimples were huge.

"All righty, Lylice, that's enough. We've got to move on. Just like the Native Americans had to. Besides, they are being taken care of now. Out on their reservations."

"*What?* Reservations doesn't mean being taken care of. It means putting them all by themselves and separating them from the rest of us. It's like segregation! Shame on the government!"

"Yeah!" said some boys.

"Whoo-hoo!" said Hannah and Debbie and some other girls.

Coach gulped. "Lylice," he said, his eyes shifting around the room. People were starting to whisper and giggle in little clumps. "Take your seat. Now."

"The United States government are crooks!" I yelled. People cheered and whistled. There was a knock at the door. Principal Harrington opened it and peeked in.

"Oh, hi, Mr. Harrington," said Coach.

Harrington walked in and stood next to me. "Excuse me," he said. No one listened. People were giving each other high-fives and shouting and whoo-hooing. I stood next to Harrington, watching it all happen. Coach was telling people to relax. Luckily, I saw Harrington put his whistle in his mouth and I put my hands over my ears. He blew it once. Ouch! People quieted down.

"Excuse me. Sixth-graders, maybe we need a special detention for this group." People groaned and shushed each other. "That's what I thought. Now, I will not tolerate this rowdy behavior. Those who were out of control will be punished. Coach Zito will explain to me"—I felt Harrington glance at my headdress out of the corner of his eye—"what happened in here today." He went on about striving for excellence and how he did not run a school full of monkeys in a zoo.

"Lylice was just setting Coach straight," said Mike Black.

"Raise your hand, boy," growled Harrington. Then Mike raised his hand but Harrington didn't call on him. "Now, Coach, if this group shows you any more rowdy behavior, let me know."

"I will," said Coach, who looked shorter than I remembered.

"And she was right," said Mike. Every head in class turned to the back row. He shrugged. "She was," he said. Harrington's nose twitched and the veins on his neck looked like they might pop out.

"Mr. Black," said Coach. "You heard Principal Harrington. Raise your hand next time. Are you prepared to get up and present?"

"Nope," he said. He gathered his camouflage bag, stood up, and strolled out the door. Harrington turned and practically ran out after him.

"Another zero for Mr. Black," said Coach, shaking his head and marking in his grade book. "Lylice. Sit," he said.

I could barely move. I tore off my headdress. The bell rang just as Coach announced an extra-credit project. It had to have a geography theme, and it had to be turned in by the end of the quarter. His words did not seem to match the way his face looked. Like he'd just been told that he was *un*invited to a party or a dance.

My blood boiled for the rest of the day. Coach was wrong. He was teaching us exactly what our books said. But the *books* were wrong! *Living in Our World* was published in 1990! Did teachers think we couldn't just flip to the front and look at the copyright date? How can you learn about history and current events from an old book?

After the final bell, I went up to the big map in Ballot Hall. I still had time before my dad came. Kids were shouting outside. Inside, there was the buzzing of the long, white lights, and I could hear Mrs. Lanza laughing somewhere, all the way down the hall. But it was mostly quiet.

Way down somewhere, right after Coach's comment about the Indian reservations, an idea had started brewing. I didn't know what it would end up being, but it was conceived. And then, in front of the map in Ballot Hall, without any thought or warning, the idea was born. I dug through my brain-on-wheels and retrieved a thick, black permanent marker.

I crossed out *United States* and wrote *Native Lands*.

The marker squeaked as I dragged it across the map.

I *X*-ed out *Mexico* and wrote *Aztec Empire*.

The strong smell of the ink made my eyes water. Sweat dotted my upper lip.

Over *Tucson* I printed *Hohokam Headquarters* in clear, capital letters.

You edit me, Harrington, I edit you.

The lights buzzed. Mrs. Lanza was still laughing. No one had seen me. I unzipped my brain-on-wheels and . . . Down the hall, Harrington stepped out of his office. A wave of terror came over me. His back was to me, and he was talking to Mrs. Lanza. She was facing in my direction, but Harrington blocked her from seeing me.

He was turning around!

I dropped the marker and ran into the nearest hiding place.

The boys' bathroom.

I didn't know what else to do. I stood right behind the door. Footsteps came closer. Closer. And closer. They stopped right outside the boys' bathroom. Right in front of the map.

"Oh, dear God . . . ," I heard him say. "Lylice?" The door to the gym opened and he yelled, "Lylice!" My name echoed.

He hadn't seen me. It was a good thing school was out and no actual boys were in the boys' room. I ran past the sinks to a door that said SPRINKLER on it. I twisted the knob like mad but it was locked. What if he came in here?

I bolted into the last stall and crouched next to the toilet. I held my nose because of the yucky smell. I was breathing too fast and loud.

And then he burst in. I pressed my lips together and held my breath.

"What am I going to do with her?" he said. Then he started to laugh. Or was he *crying?* "Oh, dear God . . . I just don't know." He went into a stall.

There was a zipping sound, then a gas noise, and then a waterfall. Thank goodness he only came in to use the restroom. I was still safe. I kept my nose plugged. Maybe he'd just go to the bathroom and leave. Wait a minute.

I was in the *same room* with Principal Harrington, and he was *going to the bathroom.*

Wait until I told Mexico! I knew my face was as red as tomato sauce. No matter how hard I tried, I could not help it. Short blurts of laughter came out of me. I couldn't control them.

"Excuse me," he said. The waterfall stopped and there was the zipping sound again, and then silence. He started to breathe hard. Not breathe, pant.

I bit my lip to stay quiet. I squeezed my nose with my thumb and pointer finger.

"Lylice Martin . . . ," he said. And then he sneezed. And sneezed. And sneezed again. He clomped into a faraway stall and ripped toilet paper off the roll. Then he blew his nose. My heart was pounding. Only a door that said SHELBY EATS IT protected me from his wrath.

"Unacceptable behavior, Lylice. Absolutely. Unacceptable. In my office. *Now.*" Footsteps clanked to the bathroom door and it swung open and shut. I let out a long breath. I pushed the thought that he hadn't washed his hands out of my head. There were bigger fish to fry. Fish that started with a *d-e-t-e-n* and ended with a *t-i-o-n*.

I dragged my brain-on-wheels to his office, staring at the carpet the whole way down the hall. I knew what I did was wrong, but I couldn't help it. That map was wrong.

Harrington gave me detentions on Wednesday,

Thursday, *and* Friday of the next week. I knew he'd give me another detention, but three? Great. Triple great. Just what I needed: three more hours sitting in silence watching him call people and look at papers. Preposterous. How was that supposed to make me learn anything?

Mrs. Lanza, who was making copies in the supply office, walked me halfway down the Ballot Hall steps.

"Don't worry, Ms. Martin, never fear," she said, her arm around my shoulder. "College is on the horizon. High school will be a chore, but college, sweet, sweet college, is only six short years away."

"Thanks, Mrs. Lanza," I said. But it didn't make me feel better. Three hours of detention with Harrington seemed like forever. I didn't even want to think about how long six years seemed.

Moseying down the steps of Ballot Hall, I heard the American flag on top of our school flapping in the wind. A drop of pride crept into my worries. Even though I had three more detentions, I felt like a conquistador for truth. Even Tony Frizell had cheered after my presentation. And Mike Black defended me.

Mexico would be so proud when I told her about the map!

My suitcase clunked behind me, like a tired old steed. The Tucson sun was starting to sink behind the Great Lawn trees, and I headed for our car, which was waiting on the horizon. As I flung open the passenger door, I decided that Mike Black was *not* the meanest boy in school.

The Snooper

Something lucky happened at my final detention.

The Wednesday and Thursday ones were terrible. Each one was a fat, boring hour of silence. On Wednesday, Harrington even made me skip band and scrub the Ballot Hall wall where the map used to hang, using lemon juice and warm water. He wanted it to be clean before he hung the new map. My fingers stayed pruney for practically two days.

On Friday, I arrived right after band. The office smelled like tuna fish.

"Hi, Lylice . . . ah . . . ah-choo!" Principal Harrington wiped his nose with a crumpled tissue.

"Bless you," I said as I slid into the small desk chair. His phone rang.

"Darn it! Thank you, Lylice. Excuse me. Yes?" he said. "This is he." Harrington nodded. "What . . . ?" he said, rustling through some papers. "No, I have you down for *next* Friday at this time." He held up a crinkly sheet. "You're out front?" He laid his head on his desk. "No. No, no. Not a problem," Harrington said. "I'll be right out."

He slammed down the phone, grumbling to himself that he *needed* a damn secretary to help him schedule interviews *for* a damn secretary. He stood up and pulled three tissues from a box on his desk, balled them up, and stuck them up his jacket sleeve at his wrist.

"Sorry your day is not going—"

Harrington shot his arm straight out, and his stiff, open palm faced me. I pressed my lips together.

"Urgh," he growled, gritting his teeth. After opening three drawers, he found a clipboard and a yellow writing tablet.

"Um . . . if this is a bad time, I can definitely—"

"Lylice! Now, don't start. Just sit. And think."

And he was gone. I swallowed. I had already had two hours to think about what I did to that ancient

map in Ballot Hall, which would hopefully be re-
placed by an *accurate* world map. After I was pretty
sure he wasn't coming back (fifteen minutes into the
hour), I pushed back my chair, stood up, and tiptoed
across the office. The door was ajar. He could walk in
with no warning.

But it was now or never.

Harrington's garbage can overflowed with dirty
tissues. The fishy smell was definitely stronger at the
desk. I had to work fast. I sifted through Post-Its and
index cards. There was a list of students' names, and
red, blue, or gold stars next to them. I had a blue
star. Nathan and Gorpat had gold ones. Hmmm. Bell
schedules. End-of-quarter doughnut party pastry
lists.

Folders were packed so thick with papers that the
whole thing looked like it was in no order at all. Harrington could use *two* damn secretaries. My heart
pounded. He could come back at any time. The life
of a conquistador!

The more I snooped, the bolder I got. I opened
drawers, looked through folders. A paper that said
Trailblazer Award nominees caught my eye. Sari

Henderson was the only name on the list. *How do you get nominated for the Trailblazer Award?*

My fingers shook as I fidgeted through the desk. A small Post-It note had the website www.findamate.com written on it. Was Harrington looking for love? My heart melted, in spite of myself.

What if he came in right now and saw me at his desk? I would be expelled and sent back to Catalina, if they'd even have me. I was damaging my future. I pricked up my ears and listened as hard as a wolf so I could hear Harrington before he burst through that door.

Aha.

Susan B. Anthony Middle School stationery. Tons and tons of it in Harrington's bottom drawer. Score! I grabbed a stack. Envelopes, envelopes, were there envelopes? Yes! I took some.

"Ah . . . ah-choo! Ah-choo!"

Sneezes from out in the hall. I was stunned. My heart stopped beating. I slammed the bottom drawer shut and made a mad dash to the small desk!

Harrington burst in. Somehow, a very unpleasant conversation floated in with him. He shook his head,

106

threw his clipboard onto his desk, and blew his nose. The stationery sat on my knees, the small desk covering it.

"Lylice," he said, rubbing his forehead and tossing a tissue into the garbage. "You can leave early. Detention cut short. See you Monday." He slumped in his chair.

"Oh, thank you, Mr. Harrington. Have a nice weekend," I said.

"You too."

Last year, at parent-teacher conferences, Mrs. Garrison had told my parents that I was trustworthy. So far this year, I had defaced school property *twice,* and now, I'd *stolen from my principal.* I unzipped my brain-on-wheels and shoved in the goods. I wondered what Mrs. Garrison would say if she knew what a renegade I had become this year. Still, if all of my punishments were like my Friday detention, I'd deface the school more often.

Sleeping in the Garden

The other houses on Hawaii Street were boring compared to Mexico's pink house. After detention number four, my dad dropped me off for a sleepover.

My very first sleepover.

"Bean, don't tell Mom I said this, but don't let the detentions stop you." My dad's teeth were the best part of him. He was a person that you had to listen to. Not just because he had good things to say, but because you couldn't take your eyes off his teeth's fang-like confidence. He was teaching a class at the University of Arizona that semester called Peaceful Solutions.

"Keep fighting the good fight," he whispered. "But keep in mind, there are other ways to make statements. Try doing something positive to make a point, rather than something negative, like, say, damaging something." He gave me a stern look. Then it was gone. "Know what I mean, Bean?"

"Know what you mean," I said.

"Have fun," he said, and leaned in to kiss my cheek.

I climbed out of the car and waved once I got up to the door. On the porch I stood next to a pink table and chairs. MENDOZA was painted above the doorbell. Each letter was a different creepy-crawly bug.

Miss Mendoza answered and gave me a big hug. In the kitchen, cholla cactus flowers were painted on top of the table. And there was one big rainbow that stretched over the cupboards.

"Holy moly," I said, twirling around without meaning to. "Miss Mendoza, you're a *real* painter!" I said. She and Mexico giggled. Mexico's aunt wore a flowered dress and sandals. Her hair was the same color as Mexico's, and her eyes were oval shaped.

"The paintings are gorgeous," I said. "Thank you for having me over, Miss Mendoza. Mexico, can I see your room?" Mexico nodded.

"Mexico, *chica,* don't forget, *hablamos con tú Papá esta noche, sí?"*

"*Sí,*" said Mexico.

"*Bueno,*" said Miss Mendoza. "Leelas, do you like Mexican food?"

"*Sí,*" I said. "*Mucho.*"

Miss Mendoza smiled. "*Que bueno,*" she said, and went into the kitchen.

You had to walk through Miss Mendoza's room to get to Mexico's. There were three small vanilla candles burning on a little table by Miss Mendoza's bed. A statue of Mary, the mother of Jesus, stood next to them. And the walls . . .

"Oh . . . ," I said. There were perfect little white daisies painted all over Miss Mendoza's light blue walls.

"I helped," said Mexico, waving me into her room.

Mexico's room was a tiny bit bigger than her aunt's, but it was still a pretty small room. There was a twin bed, a night table, and a plastic crate. And the walls!

"Oh . . . Mexico, they're . . . tremendous," I said.

My mouth hung open. Huge pink, red, and yellow flowers seemed to float along each of the four walls. It wasn't *that* small.

"You get to sleep in a garden," I said. Mexico's dimples filled her face.

Bottles of nail polish and perfumes sat on the bed-side table. Next to that stuff was an old photo in a pink frame. A man with a mustache standing with a pretty woman. A sign behind them said MI CASA ES SU CASA. The woman had huge dimples, and she wore red butterfly barrettes.

On the crate in the corner, a couple of toothpaste-looking tubes lay on some paper. Mexico showed me two of her paintings. One was a black dog on green grass. The other was a man with a mustache waving from a car. Mexico's paintings made you feel like you weren't just looking at them, you were in them.

"Mexico Mendoza," I said. "Holy moly . . ."

She shrugged. "I like to paint," she said. She pointed to the black dog. "Pocho."

"Awww," I said. "Is that your dad?" I asked, pointing to the man. Immediately I wished I hadn't. What if she didn't want to talk about him?

She nodded. She stayed looking at the painting for a minute. I took my toothbrush and pajamas out of my brain-on-wheels.

"You have to keep painting. You're so good at it." She smiled and put her paintings back on the crate. I brought out my treasure: the stationery.

"How did you get it?" she asked, her eyes twinkling. We climbed onto her bed. I told her all about my detention.

"Thank goodness for that surprise interview. Or else I wouldn't have found these," I said, handing her a sheet of the stationery. "We'll write letters to parents, and—"

"Wait a minute," Mexico said. "Leelas . . ." She looked up at the ceiling. "Okay," she said. Her eyes got really thin and squinty. "Why can't *mi tía* have the interview?" she whispered. I thought about it.

"Well, your aunt has a job. At the Andersons'," I said. Mexico sighed. "What?" I asked.

"Maria is quitting," she said.

"Why?"

"I don't know. I think it's bad there," she whispered.

"Bad how?" I asked.

"I don't know. But she always says she feels sorry for them," Mexico said, shrugging. We stared at each other. Thinking. I bit my lip. Mexico fiddled with the pleats in her red skirt.

"Okay," I said. "Here's the plan."

She closed her door all the way and we huddled together on the bed.

"We type your aunt a letter," I whispered. "It'll be from Harrington. And it'll say to come and interview to be his secretary," I said. Mexico nodded. This was the most radical thing I had ever thought of doing in my whole entire life. Ever. "I mean, if his interview schedule is all messed up, he won't know the difference, right?"

"Right," said Mexico. Her face lit up.

"I mean, she'd have to work for Harrington," I said. "But it's better than nothing."

Mexico nodded. *"Conquistadores!"* she said, lifting a fist into the air.

"Chicas!" Miss Mendoza called.

Mexico froze. "What if she heard the plan?" she whispered. "She can't know we will write the letter . . ."

"A comer!"

"Dinner," Mexico said. "Just dinner. Come on." We filed into her aunt's room, swelling with the great idea we'd just stumbled onto.

"I'll be right there," said Mexico, heading into the bathroom.

We had Miss Mendoza's chili relleno, and it was delicious. Green peppers and different kinds of cheeses all rolled up in this yummy dough, with salsa, sour cream, and guacamole on top. I noticed Mexico didn't put any of that stuff on hers.

"Mmmm . . . it's so good, Miss Mendoza," I said.

"*Gracias, chica.* I'm glad you like it," she said.

We started talking about school, and my and Mexico's grades. And I found out that Miss Mendoza loved going up to Bear Mountain too. I had an idea.

"Let's say . . . if Mexico gets honor roll this quarter, we all *have* to climb Bear Mountain. Let's make a promise. You could sleep over on the last day of the quarter, Mexico, and we could go that weekend!"

"Sounds good, Leelas. I promise," said Mexico. "I hope I can do it." Miss Mendoza nodded. I tried to bring up Miss Mendoza's job without sounding tacky.

"So, how are things over at the Andersons', Miss Mendoza? I've been in school with Hannah since I was in kindergarten," I said, trying to sound really normal.

"Oh, Leelas, it's all right," she said, grinning. "But I think I might be looking for something different soon. Something more fun," she said.

Mexico and I exchanged worried glances. I didn't know if being Principal Harrington's secretary would necessarily be *fun,* but it would be something. I knew it was against the rules to forge a note, but it was for such a good cause. It had to work.

"Well," I said, "a lot of times, something that you never thought would be fun, turns out to be . . . fun."

"Yes," said Miss Mendoza. "You're right. Life is always surprising us, *sí?*" Mexico and I nodded.

"Yeah, and sometimes something happens just at the right time, too," I said. "Like a job interview or something." Mexico kicked me under the table. I clamped my mouth shut, tight.

"You are right, Leelas. You have such a great attitude," said Miss Mendoza.

"Thank you. I just think it's not fair that it can

take so long to get citizenship and everything," I said, sipping my water.

Miss Mendoza looked surprised. Uh-oh. That was too out of the blue. Even Mexico looked at me funny. I was pushing it too hard. "I agree with you one hundred percent, *chica,*" Miss Mendoza said. "For some people it can take longer. For some shorter."

"Why?" I asked.

"I don't know, Leelas. I wish I knew. My brother, Mexico's papa, wants to come, but he is very afraid he will not get citizenship. And therefore get sent back. You know how it is with those kind of things. I was lucky. I got a visa. But soon it will run out," she said, and made the sign of the cross.

"Well, the whole thing makes me want to photo-copy my birth certificate and give it out to everyone from Mexico that comes here. I mean, come on, as long as you're working and doing something, it's not fair that you don't get benefits and health insurance and tax refunds—"

They just stared at me. If my dad were here, he'd ask me a bunch of opposing questions. But this wasn't a debate. I was talking about their lives. Their *real* lives. Not just dinner conversation.

116

"I'm sorry," I said. Darn it! "I shouldn't have said—"

"It is okay, Leelas. It is all true," said Miss Mendoza. "So, *chicas,* tonight I am making *helado frito.* Fried ice cream. Sound good?" Mexico and I nodded.

"Leelas, you will never tell that the ice cream is sugar-free," she said. "I promise."

We finished our meal. Miss Mendoza told us not to worry about cleaning up. She started to clear the table and ran water in the sink. I wondered if she had come here by herself when she was younger, like Mexico did.

"Thank you for dinner. I really loved it," I said as Mexico and I brought our plates to the sink. "And I'm sorry . . ." I said.

"Leelas, it is okay. Really," said Miss Mendoza, taking my plate and putting her hand on my shoulder.

In Mexico's room, we got into our pajamas. She painted my nails the same red as hers.

"Mexico," I said as she started my left hand. "I'm asking Nathan Shelby to the Halloween Sock Hop. I'm just going to do it."

There. It'd been floating around in my head for days, and I finally got it out.

"What?" Mexico squeaked. "Really?" she asked. I nodded. "Brave," she said. "I want to ask to the Sock Hop . . . Gorpat."

"Gorpat? Gorpat Geetha? You like Gorpat Geetha?"

"Leelas. Don't move or I will paint all over you," she said. "So what," she added.

"It's nice. I just didn't think . . ." I stopped and thought about it. Gorpat was quiet. Mexico was sort of quiet, before you got to know her. Maybe Gorpat got less quiet the more you got to know him, too. "Mexico, you should ask him. You should! Why not?"

"No, Leelas, not me," she said, shaking her head.

"Mexico!" Miss Mendoza called.

"*Sí?*" Mexico yelled.

"*Su papá!*"

"Be right back," she said, running out of her room. I felt bad for being there when her dad called from so far away. But he wasn't so far on the map, which probably made it even harder. I lay back on Mexico's bed and blew on my nails, which looked perfect. Soon there was a knock on the door. I stood up.

"Come in," I said.

"Hi, Leelas. Dessert," said Miss Mendoza. "Fried ice cream." She held two huge mugs in her hands.

"*Muchas gracias,* Miss Mendoza!"

"*De nada.* And, Leelas, you can call me Maria." She left and I tasted my first fried ice cream. Bliss. A warm, crunchy shell drizzled with something sticky sweet over scoops of vanilla ice cream.

Pretty soon Mexico came back. "Mmmm," she said, picking up her mug and spooning a bite into her mouth. "Do you love it, Leelas?" she asked. I nodded.

Oh, it was good. Maria was right. It tasted *very* sugary.

"How's your dad?" I asked after a minute of eating.

"He is okay," Mexico said. "Lonesome."

Over the rest of the night, she told me the story of taking this hot bus from Nogales to Tucson. It was full of babies and mothers, really old men by themselves, tall and strong-looking young men, and a few other kids our age who were alone, like Mexico. They were stopped by the Immigration people four times in the three-hour ride. But it turned out that they all had the correct papers to pass.

"So. Is the United States what you thought it would be like?" I asked. We lay side by side in her tiny bed.

"I did not know anything what it would be like. Except that my father said I had to go. And that he was not going. But . . ." She turned onto her side. "It is better than I thought. *Buenas noches.*"

"Buenas noches. Hasta mañana."

The wind outside made a tree's shadow dance on Mexico's wallflowers. There was a little hum in the quiet. A vanilla-strawberry scent from Maria's candles floated into Mexico's room.

"Mexico," I whispered, "your aunt will become the new secretary. I know she will."

"I hope," she whispered.

In a few minutes, she breathed beside me in rhythm. I turned onto my side as quietly as I could. Then back onto the other side. The bed was a little squeaky. Soon Mexico snored softly. I peeled the covers off, tiptoed around the bed, and opened the door a teeny bit. Except for one of the little candles still flickering, it was dark in Maria's room. I headed for the bathroom.

Little creepy-crawly bugs were painted along the bottom of the purple bathroom walls. There was a small walk-in shower with giant pink flower stickers at the bottom. Maria's and Mexico's toothbrushes were in little frog holders that were stuck to the tiles behind the faucets.

There were two pens that sat on a tiny stool between the sink and toilet. One said *Lantus* and the other said *Humalog*. I looked at them harder and figured out that they weren't pens. They were shots. Needles. These were probably how Mexico gave herself insulin. Everything I saw made me love her more.

Just as I was about to go back into her room, I heard Maria's voice.

". . . *una amiga de Mexico* . . ." she said. She was talking too fast for me to understand every word. ". . . *una amiga comica* . . ." said Maria. She laughed. I held my breath.

Amiga meant "friend."

Comica . . . must've meant funny. Maria thought I was funny! I shouldn't have been standing there listening. I should've gone right back into Mexico's room. But I stood smiling in the dark, straining to hear more.

"Miguel . . . no quiero seguir trabajando . . . Mrs. Anderson . . . dejó . . . pronto . . ."

Maria's voice wasn't happy anymore. Spanish vocabulary was whizzing through my brain. I wanted to understand. Maybe Miguel was Mexico's papa?

Paying attention in Spanish was paying off. *No trabajando* meant "not working." *Pronto* meant "soon."

". . . la insulina es muy costosa . . ."

Insulin.

The cost of insulin.

It sounded bad. A minute of quiet went by. Maria lowered her voice even more and I dared to walk closer to her bedroom door, which was open. But then I heard her coming. I scampered into Mexico's room and slid into the squeaky bed. I heard Maria close her bedroom door all the way.

My heart thumped. Mexico was still curled up on her side, snoring. She didn't hear Maria. I hoped she *never* heard her saying that kind of stuff. I turned onto my side. And back to the other side.

What if Maria just couldn't afford the insulin anymore? Would Mexico have to go back to Nogales? Our plan would work. It *would*. We were trying to do something positive, like my dad said. If Maria was hired at Susan B. Anthony, it would give her some more money and maybe even health insurance.

I lay there for a long time, going over our plan again and again. I'd type the letter and mail it to the pink house.

I turned over again and faced the couple in the MI CASA ES SU CASA picture. *Hi, Miguel,* I thought. I scooted closer to Mexico so our backs were touching.

My very first sleepover.

Greetings, Ms. Mendoza,

How are you? I am doing fine. Mexico is doing very well in her classes. With a B average, I am pretty sure she will make honor roll this quarter. I am really happy that she is going to school at Susan B. Anthony this year.

There is a situation at the school that I am trying to fix. I am looking to hire a new school secretary, and I would like to ask you something. Can you come in to interview on Monday, November 2 at 3 p.m.?

We understand that you are fluent in both English and Spanish and, due to the

high number of Spanish-speaking students
at Susan B. Anthony, we think you would
make a fabulous candidate for the job.
Your contract would include health insurance for you and your family, just like all
the teachers get.

If you can come to the interview please
sign below, and send this letter to school
with Mexico. I look forward to seeing you
on November 2 at 3 p.m.

Sincerely,

C. Harrington III, Principal

Yes, I will be there on
November 2 _____

SUSAN B. ANTHONY MIDDLE SCHOOL,
Home of the Trailblazers
www.susanb.edu

When I Am Brave

On Monday, Mexico went to the bathroom four times during two class periods. She had forgotten to bring her lunch to school, so Mrs. Lanza gave her a peanut butter sandwich.

"Mexico," I said, once she joined me at the red table. "Um, are you all right? You went to the bathroom—"

"Yes," she said. "Fine." She unwrapped her sandwich with shaky hands. "I just have to . . . go a lot today," she snapped.

But she wasn't fine. Mexico was never snippy like that. She was acting weird, and her eyes were so droopy it looked like she would fall asleep any second.

And then Mexico fell backward, off the red bench.

"Mexico!" I screamed. "Oh my God!" She landed on her bottom and then fell onto her back. I stood up with my hand over my mouth. One minute we were side by side eating, and the next, she was hitting the floor.

"Oh, help, *please!*" I screamed. I bent down and put my hands under her arms and tried to lift her up but she was too heavy. "Oh no," I cried. "*Heeeeeelp!*" I yelled, louder.

Harrington ran over with Coach behind him.

"What happened, Lylice?" asked Harrington, kneeling down by Mexico.

"I don't know. She fell off!"

Gorpat Geetha came and stood next to me, biting his nails. Kids gathered around and stared.

An ambulance came. My best friend was carried out of the cafeteria on a stretcher. Me, Sari Henderson, Gorpat, Nathan, and most of the Susan B. Anthony Middle School band stood on the Great Lawn, watching them drive away with her. Harrington stood at the curb with his head down.

"What happened to her?" I asked.

Sari put her arm around my shoulder. "The paramedics are figuring out what's wrong, and they're going to make Mexico well."

Gorpat stood still, chewing on his nails. He stopped for a second and said, "We should make her a banner or something." He went back to chewing, then stopped again. "Or something good to eat." Then he chewed some more.

"Yeah," said Nathan. "We should."

"Good call, Gorpat. Let's organize it at student council," said Sari.

"Can I help?" I asked.

"Of course," said Sari. "There's a meeting today after school in Mr. Schvitter's room," she said.

I nodded.

"Don't worry," she said. "Everything will be okay." She gave me a hug and started back up the Ballot Hall stairs. Sari was smart. I remembered what she had said to me in the bathroom the day I threw up on Tony Frizell. That it's all a part of life. But what if Mexico died? Was that part of life?

It happened too fast. I didn't get it. I wanted to

know everything, everything in the world about diabetes. Her B.S. must have been completely bonkers. Bone. I was responsible. I let Maria down. And Señora Schwartz and Mr. Harrington.

Could you die if the sugar in your blood didn't do its job? I guessed you could get really tired. So tired that you could fall over in the middle of lunch. But would your heart get so tired that it stopped beating? That was what I needed to know. I had important research to do. I doubted Mexico would be able to do homework at my house today.

Mr. S. gave me a big hug before math. I couldn't concentrate on the division lesson. How many times does 8 go into 24? *Mexico.* How many 7s are there in 49? *Mexico.* What's 500 divided by 5? It's 100: *Mexico's healthy B.S. number.*

In the most secret place, down in the basement of my soul—the place where Nathan Shelby kissed me, and where Principal Harrington nominated me for the Trailblazer Award, and where Tony Frizell stopped hating me—I pleaded to God.

Oh God, please, please let Mexico be okay. I don't know what I would do without her.

In band I kept playing B flats instead of B naturals (first fingering instead of second). Ms. McGriff called me to the podium and asked me if I'd like to pack up early. She smiled and whispered that she knew Mexico would be fine. But how could she know? I put my French horn in its case while Ms. McGriff worked with the clarinets and flutes on trills. Nathan whispered: "Lylice." I turned around.

"She'll get better," he said, his blue eyes shining. "And," he added, "I, uh, saw the old map in the office." He grinned. "You made Harrington really mad." His teeth were whiter and more perfect than ever. I tried to smile.

In Harrington's office, I called my dad's cell phone. He said he'd leave class to come get me. Harrington put his hand on my shoulder.

"Lylice," he said, "Mexico's going to be just fine. Please send her our best." I nodded and rushed out of the office. I trampled down the Ballot Hall steps with my brain-on-wheels, and my dad pulled right up. He took me to the hospital.

At the end of a long hallway, I spotted Maria.

"What's her B.S.?" I shouted before we reached her.

"Lil, don't yell," my dad whispered. "We're in the hospital." I ran to her, dropping the pink carnations he had bought.

"Leelas!" she said. She reached out her hands and I took them. Her face was red and she held a tissue.

"Her blood sugar, her blood sugar! What's the number?" I asked.

"It's back down, Leelas. It's back down," she said, making the sign of the cross.

"That's good . . ." I said. My lip was shaking.

My dad caught up to us and put his arm around Maria.

"Was it up really high?" I asked.

"Oh, yes, Leelas. It was . . . it was," she said. She knelt down and I did too. All of her words were broken up with tears. "She stopped . . . taking the insulin. She had no more left! If she doesn't take it, then . . ." *Then what?* I wanted to scream. But Maria was sobbing. My dad knelt down by us, and we just waited until she could stop.

My dad put his arm around her and gave her a squeeze. My lip shook, but I found some bravery.

"Maria," I said, swallowing. "I am so, so sorry about Mexico. I was sitting right by her . . ." I knew

131

if I looked at my dad I would bawl. "I wasn't able to help," I said. "But whatever happens, she will have been the best, best, best, best, best, best friend I ever had."

"Oh, Leelas, Mexico will get better. Don't you worry, *chica*. This . . . this was my fault." Maria gasped. "I think she feels guilty to tell me, because I have left my job, and—" She covered her face with her hands. "My brother . . . he trusted me . . . and . . ."

"It's not your fault, Miss Mendoza," my dad said. "You're doing your best." Grownups always knew the right things to say. "You let us know if you need anything," he said. Maria's eyes filled up again. She nodded, and made the sign of the cross again.

"Thank you for coming," she said. "I am so sorry." She wiped her cheeks and slowly stood up. My dad and I did too. He handed her the flowers. She smiled.

"Can I go in and see her?" I asked.

"I'm sorry, Leelas. They won't even let me go in right now. Why don't you go home, and we will call you tomorrow, okay?"

"But I want to see her," I said.

"Bean, look," said my dad. We peeked through the window. Mexico looked just like a normal, sleeping person. That made me feel good, but the frustration of not understanding everything made me feel suffocated.

"I promise we'll call you tomorrow, okay?" Maria asked.

"Okay," I said.

She knelt down in front of me. "Do you know Mexico has been okay here because of you, Leelas?"

I knew *here* meant here, Arizona, and not *here, hospital.*

"Do you know I have been okay here because of Mexico?" I asked.

Dear Nathan,

Thank you for your call. Mexico is doing better. But not great. That was very considerate of you to ask how I'm doing, even though I'm not the person who fell off the bench and fainted. My dad says

133

when things are hard, remember all of
the good things. But good things are hard
to remember when your best friend is in
the hospital.

But as long as I am in a remembering-
things mood, remember how they made us
dive for caramels at swimming lessons?
And how when I had the stomach flu
once and couldn't go, you came over after
swimming lessons with a caramel for me?
I still remember that.

W/B/R/S/P (means "Write back really
soon please"),

Lylice Martin

P.S. Even if your dad asked you to call me,
and you didn't think of it yourself, it was
still nice.

P.P.S. Do you want to go to the sock hop
with me?

The Blue and Purple Purse

It was hard to be sad when your English teacher was dressed like a pioneer, with a bonnet and high-buttoned shoes. Thank goodness Mrs. Lanza came to school in costume every day from October 1 through 31. Her bulletin board, and most of the other teachers' boards, was decorated with witches and black cats and vampires. That stuff made me smile too, but it was nothing like sitting beside Mexico at the red table.

The day after she got sick, I slipped Nathan my note before English. It was the biggest note I had ever written to anyone in my whole life. For the rest of the day, I felt like I was in that dream where you go to school but you forgot to get dressed.

Gorpat came up to me at lunch and asked if, by any

chance, I could tell Mexico that he said hello. I said I would. He thanked me and went off to a seventh-grade table. Gorpat's message would definitely cheer her up.

Hannah and Debbie came up to me at lunch also.

"Tony looks fine in red," Debbie was saying.

"Debbie loves Tony!" shouted Hannah.

"Stop!" said Debbie. She looked like she wanted Hannah to keep saying it.

"Hey, Lylice," said Hannah.

Hannah Anderson never said hey to me. "Hi. Want to sit?" I asked.

"Mmm, no. We heard you messed up the map in Ballot Hall. And you got, like, five detentions or something."

"Three." I nodded. "But I was just sticking up for Native Americans and—"

"That's *so* cool. So, Lylice," Hannah said, leaning in, opening the clasp of her blue and purple purse. "Guess what I have?"

She pulled out three notes. I recognized them. Oh no.

"Give me those!" I yelled, shooting out of my seat.

"Those weren't meant for you, Hannah Anderson."
Her wrist was quicker than mine. She was also taller.

"Nope," said Hannah, "they weren't." She glanced
back at Nathan's table and waved. He waved back.
Her eyebrows raised and lowered quickly. "But I've
got them."

"Well, you shouldn't," I said. I grabbed for her
hand across the red table. Debbie clicked her teeth.
Hannah took a step back, opened her purse again,
slipped them in, and locked the clasp. I marched right
up to her, forcing down tears. She was so pretty. Her
shiny green eyes pierced me. I noticed a big blue
bruise on her arm.

"Why are you so mean?" I blurted out.

"I'm *not* mean. It's just . . . you gave these to
Nathan," she said, shrugging, "but he gave them to
me." She made me sick. I hated her real Juicy Jeans
and the smell of her beautiful hair. I hated the way
she looked at Nathan. But mostly I hated the way he
looked at her.

If I felt naked before, now it was like my skin was
pulled away, showing my heart for everyone to laugh
at. Hannah had my notes to Nathan. He *gave* them

to her. Before I could think, I was grabbing at her purse. She lifted it over my head.

"Hannah Anderson, you're a witch!" I snarled. Out of the corner of my eye, I saw Harrington and Señora chatting at the other end of the cafeteria. They hadn't heard.

"I second that," shouted Mike Black, who stood on top of his table nearby. His friends hooted. Harrington's whistle blew.

"Black! Down from there. Or you're toast!" yelled Harrington.

"Keep your undies on, Harring-buns," said Mike as he climbed down and sat at his table. They all laughed. Mike caught my eye and gave me one firm nod and a smile. I couldn't help smiling back. Hannah and Debbie went back to the yellow table. I sat for the rest of lunch staring at my half-eaten burrito combo. I used to think the school burritos were digestible, but that was before I had Maria's food. I threw my lunch away and headed out of the cafeteria.

After band I went up to Nathan.

"For some reason," I mumbled, as I packed up my horn, "Hannah has all the notes I've written to you . . ."

"What?" he asked. "She's always going through my stuff!" He put his trombone into its case and snapped the buckles closed. He rolled his eyes and let out a big sigh. "Don't worry. I'll . . . I'll get 'em back," he said.

So he didn't *give* them to her. She *stole* them.

"Nathan?"

"Yeah?"

"Did you . . . read the one . . . I gave you . . . today?" I asked.

"Yeah," he nodded. "Yeah, Lylice. That sounds all right," he said. "I, uh, I'll go to the Hop with you." He slugged my arm softly. I grinned. There went my heart, thumping like the bass drum in "Lightly Row." I broke into a sweat. My mouth went dry.

What was wrong with me? Why was I getting so nervous in front of a boy I'd known all my life? Ever since we were little and played in his backyard, I had looked up to Nathan Shelby. Ever since we made mud pies and put weeds on top for decoration. Ever since we ate bologna sandwiches on his lawn. Ever since I could remember.

He slung his backpack over his shoulder. I couldn't understand why I felt like crying. We were going on a *date*. Shouldn't I be ecstatic? I wondered about my dad's old saying about being careful what you wished for because you just might get it.

"Are you sure you want to go?" I asked. His perfect lips parted and only air slid out.

"Yeah . . . I want to," he finally said. "Of course I do." He waved and backed away. I heard the band-room door being flung open and then clasp shut.

I stood alone next to Mexico's poor tuba. It hadn't been touched since she had gone into the hospital. Two whole days. The band was left with no bass, no grounding. I loved that such a small person was the core of such huge music.

That evening, Maria called, just like she'd promised. She said that Mexico was doing much better, and that she was going home in a few days.

"Maria, why did she faint?" I asked.

She took a breath. "She got very sick with a condition."

"Was it hyperglycemia?" I remembered the term from my report on Winnie Mandela.

"Yes, Leelas, that's right. Her body was making too much sugar. Insulin helps to . . . to break down that sugar, but Mexico . . . stopped taking it."

140

"But she's never going to do that again, right?" I asked. I could hear Maria smile.

"Right, Leelas. From now on, I check her insulin every week. Make sure that she has what she needs."

"Will you tell her I miss her?"

"Yes. She misses you too."

Señora's Turn

In Spanish the next morning, we paired up to review colors. I was glad for the new lesson. And glad to be paired up with Nathan.

"*Rojo,*" I said.

"Red. *Amarillo,*" he said.

"Yellow. *Naranja,*" I said.

"Orange. *Azul,*" he said.

"Blue. Well, we know our colors by heart," I said. We started talking about the Hop.

"You could go as a piece of broccoli and I could go as a rice cooker!" I was proud of the idea. Nathan made a face.

"A *rice cooker?* Lylice, you weirdo," he said, smiling and shaking his head.

"I may be weird, but some of the greatest geniuses of our time were considered weird before they got famous," I said. "Or we could go as famous people," I said.

"That's cool," he said. "Like who?"

"Like anyone. Like Copernicus. Or Beethoven. People like that. Or anyone you want!"

Nathan nodded.

"You could go as some old, great leader. Like Winston Churchill. Or John Lennon!" I said. Nathan laughed.

"Juanita!" said Señora. *"Ven a mi escritorio, por favor. Ahora."* Hannah's mouth was frozen open, and she was staring at Debbie.

"And bring what's in your hands," Señora added in crisp English. Everyone watched Hannah push back her chair and walk slowly to Señora's desk.

Notes were in her hands.

Señora took them, smiled at Hannah, and put them in a drawer. *"Siéntate, por favor,* Juanita," said Señora pleasantly. Hannah went back to her chair, flopped down next to Debbie, and crossed her arms over her chest. Nathan and I locked eyes.

"You said—"

"I tried. But Hannah . . . Hannah's . . ." He shook his head. Hannah pouted at Nathan. He blushed.

Great. Double great. Not only had Hannah Anderson read them, and Debbie too probably, now Señora was going to read my poems to Nathan. Just great.

Into Cherryvale

On the third day Mexico was absent, my dad dropped me off at the hospital after school. I clunked down the long hallway to Mexico's room, lugging a shopping bag and carrying a poster-board card. The front said WE MISS YOU, MEXICO! in glittery flowers.

I found Mexico asleep and Maria on a chair next to her, dozing, with a tablet of paper in her lap. Mexico opened her eyes and grinned at me.

"Leelas!"

A thin tube went from her arm to a big machine. I felt myself getting sad and tried to give a cheery smile.

"Mexico Mendoza, we've got a lot of catching up to do!"

I hugged my best friend. She hugged back. It felt like morning, but it was almost four in the afternoon. Maria stood and kissed my cheek. Then she left the room. I sat in Maria's chair with a thud. It was harder than I thought it'd be.

"So. *Cómo estas?*" I asked.

"Bien," she said. "Well, not too bad."

"Have I got surprises for you. Look!" I held up the card for her. She grinned. Her eyes were heavy though, and she blinked a few times.

"The whole entire school signed it. You can read it later," I said, putting it against the wall. "And Gorpat made you dumplings and plum sauce." She smiled bigger. "*And* he said to tell you hi." Her dimples came out. "And I . . ."

I was going to give her the gift I'd found for her at the mall, but she was so drowsy. I'd give it to her later. It was the most perfect present. I hoped she'd like it.

"But for now, you just rest. Just rest and rest and rest," I said, patting her hand. She nodded and squeezed my hand.

She was asleep again. I'd wanted to tell her about the notes, about Hannah and Debbie. That Nathan

Shelby had said yes. But she didn't need to know all that right now. She just needed to get better.

"She's asleep," I whispered, leaning out the doorway. "And there's a treat in the bag, from Gorpat. Should be yummy." Maria was out in the hallway on another hard chair, sipping a soda and staring at the ceiling.

"Okay, Leelas," she said, yawning. "She will probably nap for a little bit. Let me take you home. Then I'll come back for the treat."

We headed down the long, quiet hallway and out into the parking lot.

"Leelas, if you do not mind," said Maria, "I have to stop off at the Andersons'. I have some of their laundry," she said, and revved the black truck.

"Oh, great. Sure. That's fine," I said, trying to sound perky. If there was anything I wanted to do less than go to the Andersons' right then, it was go to Principal Harrington's house.

"Thanks, Leelas. I will be very quick. Promise. This will be the last time I visit the Andersons."

"No, it's fine. And thank you for the ride," I said.

"Thank you for coming to visit. She is really doing better." Maria smiled and made the sign of the cross. She went on about Mexico's wonderful doctor. We whizzed past the Desert Gardens Mall and the Catalina Library. Up the hill and into Cherryvale.

There was a black gate in front of the Andersons' house. After punching in the code, Maria pulled into the circular driveway behind the fancy blue car. The Andersons lived in a huge white, two-story house with a red door. The porch light wasn't on.

I wondered why Hannah went to Susan B. Anthony when her mother could probably afford to send her somewhere else. There were tons of private schools in Cherryvale.

"I will be right back," said Maria. "You can just wait."

She turned off the truck and got out. The sky was dark orange. It would be nighttime soon. Even though I didn't have to see her, just knowing that Hannah was right behind that red door gave me the heebie-jeebies. I sank into the front seat.

Maria was unloading bags from the back of the truck. Big bags. One thudded to the ground and the truck shook. I opened my door and got out.

"Maria, let me help you," I said. Dang it! I couldn't just sit while Maria worked.

"No, no, Leelas, I have it," she said as she rolled another bag out of the truck. "Just wait for me."

"It's okay," I said, grabbing one of the bags from her and dragging it toward the front door.

And that was when we heard groaning.

Grownups

A man lay sprawled on the Andersons' grass, right near the front steps.

I just stood there. Maria kept dragging her bag. He grabbed his stomach and babbled something. It was getting dark but I could tell his suit was flashy. Maybe even made of silk. A long splotch of something gooey globbed down the front of his shirt. He cradled a big empty bottle with a red label in his arms like a doll. It didn't seem to bother him that two people were walking around him or that he was lying outside at night. It didn't seem to bother Maria either.

Grownups don't do that. Grownups don't throw up and lie in it.

Grownups tell *kids* not to do that.

Maria rang the bell. A door slammed. Feet trampled down stairs. The porch light went on. The front door flew open.

"Maria, baby," said Mrs. Anderson, smiling. Her frizzy hair was in a ponytail. She wore a green robe and white fluffy slippers. Her green eyes were very red.

"Hannah, Jason, come down here," she called. "I've got your last check," she told Maria. A familiar smell poured out of her mouth, her clothes, the house. I knew it from volunteering at the soup kitchen. Liquor. She crossed her arms over her chest and leaned into the doorway.

"Is that Lylice? Hi, Lylice! How are *you?*"

"Fine," I said, trying to smile.

"Great," she said. "How's Mexico?"

"Better. Much better. Thank you for the flowers you sent," said Maria. "Mrs. Anderson, do you want me to come in and make you some tea, *chica?*"

"No, no. I'm . . . having tea," said Mrs. Anderson, as if her mind were thinking another thought. She tried standing without leaning into the doorway but couldn't.

"I've got your last check," she said again, pointing to Maria. "Hannah!" she yelled. "Come say hi to

151

Maria. Bring your brother," she whined. "Mommy needs help."

A door creaked. Next to Mrs. Anderson, a desk was cluttered with papers, mail, and more empty bottles with red labels. Behind us, the man mumbled to himself.

I saw Hannah before she saw me.

She walked through what looked like a den and stood next to the desk. Tearstains marked her cheeks. I straightened up. She was barefoot and wore this long, blue nightgown with thin shoulder straps. A blue bruise started at Hannah's shoulder and blotched all the way down her arm.

"Mommy, I don't *want*—" She froze in her words.

Our eyes locked.

Then she looked at her feet. I wanted to run into her house and take her out of it. I didn't want anyone, even Hannah Anderson, to live where grownups barfed on the lawn. She was a real person.

"Maria and Lylice came by to bring the . . . baggie?" slurred Mrs. Anderson, who suddenly cackled. She smoothed Hannah's hair. Hannah kept looking at her feet.

"The . . . baggie?" She kept laughing.

Grownups were not supposed to do this.

"The . . ." Mrs. Anderson trailed off. She grabbed Hannah's shoulder and leaned on her with her full weight, to steady herself. Hannah let out a cry.

"They brought the . . . ," said Mrs. Anderson.

"Laundry?" I said. Hannah's eyes watered.

"Yesssss! The *laundry!*" Mrs. Anderson kept leaning on Hannah, whose face was screwed up in pain. A little boy in airplane pajamas came around to Mrs. Anderson's other side. He held a harmonica.

"Ree-ya!" he said when he saw Maria.

"Hi, JJ," said Maria. He threw himself at her legs, hugging her. The man behind us mumbled. No one said anything about him.

"Okay, *chicas,*" Maria said, petting JJ's hair and kissing him, "I have to get Leelas home. Want to help your mom with these?" she asked Hannah.

Hannah gave Maria a dirty look. She took my laundry bag and dragged it past her mother and the desk, through the den, and then she disappeared.

"I have your last check . . . " Mrs. Anderson leaned over the desk. JJ clutched Maria and would not let go.

Hannah rushed back, grabbed the other laundry bag, and leaned it against the desk. Then she tried to pry JJ from Maria's legs. He cried that he wanted Ree-ya to stay. Hannah managed to pick him up, and she kissed him on the head. He kept bawling and slapped Hannah's back.

Hannah opened a drawer, pulled out an envelope, and handed it to Maria.

"Thank you," Maria said, her lip shaking. "You sure you don't want me to make you some tea, Mrs. Anderson?"

"No, no," said Hannah's mother. "Hannah will. And I've got your last check, Maria." Hannah glared at Maria. And then she slammed the door. Maria wiped her eyes, and we headed back to the truck. We walked across the lawn, past the man, who held his stomach and rolled from side to side.

"I just feel so sorry for those kids . . . so sorry," Maria was saying. When we got to the truck, we could still hear JJ wailing.

All the way home, I searched and searched for words. But none came. Maria didn't find any either, but tears were still going down her cheeks when we pulled into Saguaro Circle.

At home, my mom and dad had already eaten. My mom heated some leftover pasta for me. I ate a few bites and fed Meatball a meatball because she wouldn't stop meowing. Then I let her lick a spoonful of sour cream for dessert. She loved that.

After I rinsed my plate and put it in the dishwasher, I wandered into the living room with a mug of hot chocolate. I plopped down on the couch between my parents. My mom was marking a book with a yellow highlighter.

"Did you get full, Bean?" my dad asked as he shut down his laptop.

"Yeah," I said.

"You got homework?" he asked.

"Yeah."

"Glad to hear Mexico's doing well," said my mom.

"Yeah," I said.

"Are you the 'Yeah' lady tonight?" my dad asked, grinning. I sighed and shrugged my shoulders.

"Dad, can I borrow your laptop? I have research to do," I said.

"Absolutely, Bean," he said. I could feel him wanting to say something more, but he didn't. I wanted to tell them about Hannah, but I didn't.

"Mom, how on earth are they paying Mexico's hospital bills?" I asked.

"Well, they've managed this far. I'm sure they'll figure it out."

"But what if they don't?" I gulped. "What if she has to go back to Nogales or something?"

Since I met Mexico, the question had been buried under all of the relief that her friendship had given me.

"The Mendozas are doing everything they can so that Mexico stays," my mom said.

She wrapped her arm around me. We sat like that for a few minutes. Then I said good night, took the laptop in my room, and closed the door. I climbed up on my bed and turned it on. The screen saver was a photo of me holding Meatball in one hand when she was a baby.

Only twenty-six signatures on Nogales Flowers. Bringing back art was slow going. I didn't feel like worrying about it, though. I typed in *alcoholism* and *Tucson* and *help*. A bunch of places came up. Hospitals and AA meetings and rehab centers. Could

I tell Hannah about these places? Would she even listen?

I got into my pajamas. Then I went to get paper from my brain-on-wheels to write some of the places down. All that extra Susan B. Anthony stationery was still crammed in there. What a waste. Well, I'd recycle it. I thumbed through the fat stack of empty sheets. Then I stopped.

There was writing on one.

In messy cursive it said, *Dear Ms. BlackBear, I am truly sorry to hear about Mike's grandmother. I am*

It just stopped in the middle of the sentence. A paper clip was holding that *beginning* of a letter to another letter. A letter to Mr. Harrington. It was on notebook paper and the writing looked like first-grade printing. I looked down at the signature. Carol BlackBear.

Dear Mr. Herrington,

I am writing you for help. I hope I'm not bothering you. I dont know what to do. A lot has gone on for my son lately. His grandmother just died of overian cancer which is hard for Mike because he loved her. She would speak about our Iroquois heritage to him. His father dont ever do that. He has made Mike feel ashamed of it. I'm so worried about what Mike is doing. I dont see him half the time. He is so smart, Mr. Herrington I know he is. If theres someone in our family who can become something, its my son. Please dont give up on him.

Thank you,
Carol BlackBear

I held the letter to my heart. Being a grownup almost seemed harder than being a kid. I shut down the laptop and got into bed. In the dark I said, "Mike BlackBear," out loud.

A LANZA LEGACY
by Lylice Martin, Staff Writer

This month, Mrs. Eleanor Lanza—our revered English and Language Arts teacher—has donned nearly three dozen personalities! We were lucky enough to catch up with Mrs. Lanza one afternoon as she sifted through unclaimed book report dioramas.

"Halloween is a time when adults, especially, should take advantage of the permission to act like kids. It's exhilarating!" That exhilaration has conjured much talk among Susan B. Anthony Middle School students on school dress codes.

"If she gets to wear a sequined tank dress to school because she's a movie star that day, I want to, too," sixth-grader Debbie Dominguez declared, gathering her books after English.

"She shouldn't be permitted to wear all that stuff," offered Gorpat Geetha, seventh grade, as he slurped soup from a Middle-earth thermos. "It's distracting. When you're studying *The Diary of Anne Frank,* you don't want to hear about it from a bear."

"I like seeing an old lady in shorts!" says Tony Frizell, a sixth-grader.

Mrs. Lanza has dressed up every Halloween season for all of her thirty-five years of teaching. Among her favorite costumes this year were Queen Elizabeth, Medusa, a soccer player, and Rapunzel.

Happy Halloween, Susan B. Anthony Trailblazers!

Log on to:

http://nogalesflowers.blogspot.com

to post your spookiest Halloween memories and *to sign a petition!*

The Only Smile of the Day

It was the day before the Halloween Sock Hop. Quarter grades were in, and the end-of-quarter doughnut party was in full swing. Well, *party* was an exaggeration. Instead of going to sixth period, everyone came to the gym and ate doughnuts.

Harrington and Señora, who was eating a cinnamon bun, were chatting near the éclairs. Nathan, Tony, Hannah, and Debbie stood by the hot chocolate. Gorpat and some seventh-grade boys ate chocolate bars near the bleachers. Mr. Schvitter had to leave the party early, so I stood alone, eating a cruller. I saw Mike Black and his crowd huddled at the back of the gym. Mike pointed at the ceiling.

"Lylice," Hannah said. She suddenly stood in front of me.

"Hi, Hannah . . . ," I said. I swallowed. "Um," I said. I lowered my voice. "I'm sorry." I couldn't look at her. "I'm sure it's hard taking care of your brother . . . and taking care of your moth—"

"*Shut up,*" she spat, glancing sideways. "It's none of your business," she said. "So just *shut up.*"

I shouldn't have said anything. I backed away. She shuffled through her purple and blue purse and came out with pink lip-gloss. She rubbed her lips together and then cleared her throat.

"So, Nathan likes you," she said, fishing around in her purse again.

"Oh . . . ," I said.

"He told me to tell you," she said, tilting her head back and pouring in some Tangy Tarts, "that he cannot *wait* to go to the Sock Hop with you. But"—she sucked on the candy—"he said he doesn't want Mexico to go too."

"What . . . ?"

Hannah clicked her teeth. "He's just really nervous about going with you. He thinks if she's there, you'll be totally distracted."

I felt like I'd been slapped. I didn't know what to say. What was happening? We looked over at Na-

162

than. He grinned at us and slung his backpack over his shoulder. His fingers tapped on his thighs.

"So you're going to have to tell Mexico," said Hannah, shrugging.

"But why would I go with Nathan if he's making my friend not go?" I asked slowly, trying to make sense of it. My heart boomed and my cheeks burned. Something in my stomach was not right.

"Lylice, he's just *nervous*. Don't you *get* it?" she asked, rolling her eyes. "He wants to be *alone* with you," she said, suddenly smiling. "And since Mexico's sick anyway . . ."

"But she's better," I said. It was so wrong and so awful.

"Well, if you want to go with Nathan, Mexico can't go. That's just—what he said."

"I don't understand," I said.

"Lylice," she whispered, "he's shy, you know? He really just wants to be alone with you." She smiled a fresh Tangy Tart grin. She was the prettiest girl I knew personally. "Anyways, he *really* likes you. I swear." She crossed her arms over her chest. "Oh, and Lylice," she whispered, and stepped closer to me. "Sorry I stole your notes." She looked down, then right at me. "Nathan totally had a bone about it." She turned and walked back to her friends and put her arm around Debbie.

The gym got noisier. Someone screamed and people clapped. Someone let out a long burp, and kids burst out laughing. Harrington's whistle blew. Mike and his group at the back of the gym hollered and laughed. Nathan was heading to the trash. I dragged my brain-on-wheels toward him.

"Nathan," I said. "Explain to me why you don't want Mexico at the dance. Now," I said.

"Lylice . . . shhhh," Nathan said.

"I won't *shhhh*. It's preposterous and mean." I blinked away tears.

"Lylice—" Nathan stopped and glanced back at Hannah, who stared at us from the hot chocolate table. He turned to me again with a pitying look, an I-know-something-you-don't-know look.

"What? Just tell me," I begged. I thought of Nathan's older brothers and how he always used to get blamed for their dumb pranks. I remembered when they took their third stepmom's pillow out of the pillowcase and filled it with dirt. And once they put a dead cricket in her slipper. She always punished Nathan and not them. Now he looked at me with his brothers' fake-innocent eyes.

You're not mean, I wanted to say. *You're not mean like them.*

He opened his mouth and took a breath.

"What?" I asked. Hannah yelled, "Swellby Shelby, come here!" Nathan drummed his fingers on his thighs.

"Lylice, did Mexico's aunt, uh, quit as uh, Hannah's maid?" he whispered.

"What on God's green earth does that have to do with anything?" I asked. "Yes, she did."

"Okay, okay," said Nathan. "Nothing against Mexico. I *like* Mexico. I just want to, uh, be alone . . . with you," he said, staring at the floor. "So, if she, uh, wasn't there, it would be . . . probably . . . better."

"What are you *talking* about? I mean, even if Mexico's there, I'd still . . . pay attention to you," I said. A yucky feeling traveled from the pit of my stomach into my heart.

"Lylice," he whispered. "What you told me in your note . . . I remember that too. And you were wrong. The phone call was my idea." He grinned at me and stepped closer. He smelled like cinnamon. His blue eyes zapped at my heart, which burst open and lifted me right off the ground.

"So . . . just me and you at the dance?" he asked. For a second, there was no cafeteria, no doughnuts, no Hannah, no anything except for Nathan Shelby. And I got the feeling that maybe I didn't just look up to Nathan. Maybe it was something more than that.

Hannah's laugh came closer. And Debbie's. Louder and louder. They had giggled their way over.

"Sorry, Lylice, we have to borrow him!" Hannah grabbed Nathan's arm and led him over to the hot chocolate.

The final bell rang. I tossed the rest of my cruller into the trash and I headed into Ballot Hall, just as Mike Black bounded out of the boys' bathroom with his friends. He stopped while the others trampled down the hall, shouting and high-fiving. The whole school was filing out.

"Hi, Lylice Martin!" sang Mike Black. He was out of breath and held a wrench in his thick hand.

"Hi yourself, Mike Black," I said. *BlackBear*, I wanted to say.

"You going to the dance?" he asked, grinning.

Mike's cheeks puffed out when he smiled. He really did remind you of a bear. A nice one.

"Yes," I said. "Are you?" I really hoped he was.

"Yeah, I'll be there. I need a shower," he said with a wink. He trotted ahead of me, slipping the wrench into his knapsack.

For the first time all day, I smiled. Maybe the shower comment had something to do with Mike's costume. Maybe it didn't. But that was why I smiled.

In the car, I sat still, my stomach turning flips.

"Bean, you okay?" my dad asked.

"Yeah," I said.

"You sure you want to go to Mexico's?" he asked, feeling my forehead. "You don't look so good."

"Yeah. I'm sure," I said.

We turned into the Mendozas' driveway. My dad kissed my cheek. The smell of tomato salsa filled Hawaii Street. Maria sat on the pink porch, chewing a pencil, her tablet of paper in her lap. Inside, the vanilla candles in her room glowed. I knocked on Mexico's bedroom door. Maybe she *would* have to stay home and recover.

I have started to question my instincts.

Mexico's Gift

"Mexico? Can I come in?"

"Leelas! Hi!" She sat up and smiled at me, and her dimples were as deep as Grand Canyons. She was still Mexico, but even skinnier.

"Hi."

"Come and sit," she said, and she scooted over and patted the bed. Two picture books were open in front of her. One on Frida Kahlo, and one on Diego Rivera. I sat.

"Okay. Leelas, do you want to know what?" she asked, her eyes twinkling and her hand on top of mine. "Maria and I are making my costume for I can go to the Hop tomorrow!"

"Oh . . . !" Words got stuck in my throat. "Be right back."

"Okay," she said. I headed out of her bedroom and into Maria's bathroom.

Kneeling at the toilet, I threw up pink cruller. That damned doughnut party. I wiped my face and swallowed some cold tap water. My insides still burned. The face in the mirror was not really mine. My hands weren't mine. I tried to wash the meanness off them. I walked back in and sat on Mexico's bed.

"Leelas, you okay?" she asked, making a face. "You look green."

"I'm really quite fine. I've got something very important to discuss with you," I said. I stood.

"Okay," she said.

"The Hop. There's been a situation, regarding the—Halloween Sock Hop."

I was pacing in her room, which meant two steps one way, two steps the other. Two steps one way, two steps the other. I folded my hands together because I didn't know what to do.

"The school has sent me over with—some disappointing news. The school said that you must remain here, in your home, during the Halloween Sock Hop. The school was worried that you are not well enough—"

"But I am well. I can tell the doctor to tell them. Maria will tell them," she said. "And Leelas," she whispered, "okay, Maria is going to the appointment with Harrington. The plan is working!"

"Mexico, that's so great." My heart exploded and sank in the same second.

"But I can go to the Hop. I am going. I will go in and tell principal myself," she said. I couldn't look at her. "Leelas. Sit."

I sat. My hands were still folded tight. I couldn't do this. Mexico was the first and only best friend I had ever had. And so I told her everything: Nathan, the Hop, Hannah, the stolen notes. The note that I wrote Nathan. The one about the dance.

"Mexico, Nathan thinks if you go too . . ."

"Leelas," said Mexico. "So, it's not the school, it's you. You are telling me to not go?"

"I just thought that since you would be tired—"

"I am not tired."

Tears fell down her face like water from a drippy faucet. I had never seen her so upset. Ever. She threw off her covers and got out of bed. The Frida Kahlo book fell on the floor. I took a step back, hitting the door.

The way Mexico was crying made me scared. She stood very still and studied me, her stare going back and forth from one of my eyes to the other. And tears just fell down her cheeks. I was scared that she was still sick and that she shouldn't be getting so worked up and all. I was scared because I was the one who had made her cry.

"Everybody thinks I am *tired. I am not.* I want to go. The school did not say I cannot go, did they, Leelas. You lied to me."

I wished I would burst into flames.

"I'm sorry . . . I . . ."

"*Leelas Martin.* Leelas Martin. I cannot believe. . ." She walked to the crate and ruffled through some stuff. Then she put a painting on the bed.

It was of my room. There was Meatball's scratching post, and there was my blue canopy bed. And there was Meatball, going to the bathroom in my heat vent. The corner said, Te quiero, *Lylice-buddy, thank you for homework! Mexico Mendoza.*

My bottom lip shook like a volcano. We were face to face. I tried not to look right at her, but I did. Mexico was sick, and what was she doing? Making me a painting. I was well, and what was I doing? Tell-

171

ing her to stay home from the dance when she really wanted to go.

There was nothing right to say. "I'm s-sorry." My face felt like someone else's face and my hands started to get that prickly feeling, like right before they fall asleep. Mexico was getting over being sick and now I had made her sicker.

I swallowed, wishing I could say the magic thing that would erase the last five minutes from the universe. I ran out of her room, through Maria's, into the kitchen, and through the front door. I told Maria I was just sick, and that I needed fresh air. Too many doughnuts.

I left the painting. It was meant for a real friend.

The Sock Hop Flop

Nathan did not get the door. Three jack-o'-lanterns
flickered on the Shelbys' porch. Our car's engine
chugged at the curb. It was 6:15 p.m.

"Arrrrrrgh, Miss Lylice. Great costume. Very sophisticated!" said Mr. Shelby with some kind of Scot-
tish accent.

"Thank you. Susan B. Anthony at your service,"
I said, and curtsied. I might have felt sophisticated if
my heart hadn't been in knots. My picket signs said,
DONT' BE A DOLT—GET OUT AND VOTE! and WOMAN
AND MAN, LET'S TAKE A STAND!

"Blackbeard," he said, offering his hook, which
I shook. He'd answered the door wearing shorts, a
vest over a billowy blouse, a really thick beard, and a

monocle. The costume was good, but he hadn't taken off his Bluetooth earpiece, which sort of ruined it.

"Pleased to make your acquaintance, Mr. Beard," I said.

Mr. Shelby leaned out of the doorway and waved at my dad. "What can I do for you, me matey?" he asked.

"Is Nathan ready?" I asked.

"No . . . ?"

"Oh. Well, we're—we're dates. I asked him. And he said yes. Does he need a ride?" I heard myself ask, trying to ignore the awkwardness. There were running, hooting boys beyond Mr. Shelby. Tony Frizell was in there. I could hear him giggling. And was that *girls'* laughter?

"What?" he asked, and he pulled off his monocle. I nodded. I could feel the pot roast in my stomach wanting to come up. Swallowing hard, I tried to smile.

"Is he still getting ready?" I asked, somehow knowing that doom was inevitable.

"Well, well, well," said Mr. Shelby, dropping the act. "It looks like we've got a situation here, Lylice." He tilted his head back and yelled: "Nathan Ryan Shelby, get down here. *Now.*" It was as if Mr. Shel-

174

by bit the words off of his own tongue. The laughter within the house stopped. Now I could barely hear whispering.

I would not bring myself to glance back at my dad. A huge bowl overflowing with chocolate kisses and miniature candy bars sat beside the jack-o'-lanterns on the porch. Suddenly, there was Nathan, in the doorway behind his father.

"Ah, there he is," said Mr. Shelby. "Your date's here, Nate. Ready to go?" he asked, smirking. He grabbed Nathan's wrist and dragged him onto the porch with me.

"Hey, Lylice," Nathan said to the welcome mat under his feet.

"You want to explain what that other little girl is doing in our house? Or you want me to? I don't get it, Nathan. How can you act like such an idiot?"

Suddenly Mr. Shelby grabbed Nathan's chin and squeezed, hard. "Look at me when I'm talking to you. And *speak up,* why don't you? You know something, I used to be afraid to say my mind too, and it got me nowhere. It'll trick you into treating people like crap. Is that what you want?"

Mr. Shelby let go of Nathan, his eyes full of fire.

"What the hell are you so afraid of? Excuse me, Lylice." He stepped into the house and slammed the front door shut. The pirate was gone.

I knew what the hell *I'd* be afraid of.

Nathan seemed unfazed by his dad's outburst, but I was shocked. I'd never seen Mr. Shelby that angry.

The smell of pumpkin wound its way into the thick silence that settled between us. It was completely dark out now, and an October breeze snuck onto the porch. I shivered. Nathan stood like a statue, his face hanging toward the floorboards. He neither spoke nor seemed to breathe.

It's hard to be mad at someone and feel bad for him at the same time.

"Guess I'll see you there," I said, after a long minute. I wanted his eyes. Just to see what was in them right then. But he wouldn't give them to me. I walked back to my dad, who sat straining his neck to see Nathan's porch. I opened the door and climbed in.

"He's not ready," I said, slamming the car door. When I sat, my hoop skirt made my gown smash right into my face. The bun in my hair felt too tight, the pink lipstick too cheery. My dad revved the engine.

Silence. I could feel him wanting to say something.

"Should we wait?" he finally asked.

"No," I said. "Take me to the dance. I've got decorating to do."

"Got it," he said.

I stared out my window. Nathan's head was raised, and he was looking into the car. His feet hadn't moved, though, and as we drove away, it seemed like he'd be glued to that spot forever. Tears were somewhere down deep in me, buried like pearls.

I looked at my red fingernails. I wished so hard that things had been different. That Mexico was in the car with us. That we'd just gone to pick *her* up, and not Nathan. If I hadn't asked him to the dance, I wouldn't have had to see his father act like that. What was worse, I could see Mr. Shelby's point. But he didn't have to be so mean.

We pulled up outside Ballot Hall. The American flag danced in the crisp wind. For some reason, the marquee on the Great Lawn lit an instant fire in my chest:

BOO! HAPPY HALLO EEN

TRAILBLA ERS!

Didn't they have enough money at this school for a damn *W* and a flipping *Z*?

Inside, the gym was still the gym. Out came the black-cat cake, Cheese Chomps, punch, and soda. Inside a plastic sack with a Post-It note that said *Mendoza* on it, there was a bag of sugar-free candy. Blinking back tears, I poured the gummy worms and gummy spiders into a bowl. Then I went right over to help Mrs. Lanza with the apples. Being busy was the only way to keep everything down.

Pretty soon, black and orange streamers dangled from both basketball hoops, and jack-o'-lanterns glowed in the corners of the gym. Mrs. Lanza's huge metal bucket was so heavy with water and apples that we left it on the floor next to the snack table.

Mrs. Lanza was a sorceress, Ms. McGriff was a treble clef sign (my favorite costume of the evening), and Mr. Schvitter, our DJ, wore a red jump suit, sunglasses, and a dollar-sign medallion around his neck. His gray hair was all spiked up and looked wet.

Gorpat Geetha, who was early, was dressed as a Hobbit. He had on a funny brown hat, pointy shoes, and short pants. Sari Henderson had arrived early too, dressed as the Statue of Liberty. She wore a green dress and crown and held a homemade torch.

The "haunted house," a huge cardboard box with a door flap cut out and decorated with ghosts, was set up under one of the hoops, next to Mr. S.'s speakers. Mrs. Lanza released black helium balloons to the ceiling as kids started to arrive.

In Susan B. Anthony spirit, I set out to grant every student the right to vote, conducting several polls (best costume, student; best costume, teacher; favorite hors d'oeuvre, sweet; favorite hors d'oeuvre, salty). I'd post the results in the *Suffragette Star.* Gorpat Geetha was the first one I polled.

"You look very fine this evening, Miss Anthony." He knew exactly who I was.

"Thank you, Frodo. Or is it Bilbo?"

"Frodo," he said, and held up his gloved hands. One had only four fingers. "By any chance, is Mexico coming?"

I imagined Maria and Mexico putting together her costume. Them eating Maria's yummy homemade food. The creepy-crawlies that spelled *Mendoza* by the front door. I would never go to Mexico's again.

And for what? Nathan Shelby was coming to this dance with "that other little girl."

I have started to question trust.

"I don't know if Mexico's coming, Gorpat."

"Oh. By any chance, are you here with Nathan?"

"No," I said.

Mr. S. put on the hip-hop version of the "Hokey Pokey." People booed. They should really call it a *sit* instead of a *dance,* because that was what most kids were doing.

Except for Señora Schwartz and some man, the dance floor was empty. Señora was a lioness. She wore a tan skirt and tights and cat makeup. The man, a lion tamer, had on a top hat and a suit with tails. And was that an actual whip in his belt? I glanced around but did not see Harrington anywhere. I wondered if whips went against dress codes.

"Lyliiiiiiiiice, darling! *Hiiiiiiiiii!*"

It was Hannah Anderson. She and Debbie had clomped over in their high heels. "We just got here. Nathan's *real* excited to see you!" They both wore black tights, leotards, and kitty ears. The little pink noses and black whiskers that they'd painted on their faces were so cute I could have barfed. The smell of bubblegum nearly gassed me into unconsciousness.

"So," I said, turning back to Gorpat. "Who's your date, Frodo?"

"Ah, no one. Just me. Couldn't find anyone in the shire to take this evening!"

"Um, hel*lo,* Lylice," said Hannah. "I said Nathan's excited to see you." She smiled a fake grin. "We'll be right back!" They stamped off, giggling.

I swallowed hard. Pot roast was delicious when you were eating it the first time. But I didn't need to see it again. *Please, please stay down, please.*

"Well, that's—that's all right, Frodo. I'm sure you'll find someone nice to dance with this evening." Mexico was right: Gorpat was kind of cute when dressed as a Hobbit. I wished she were there.

"Sí, creo que sí."

Gorpat and I turned around.

"Hi."

Mexico Mendoza was dressed as Frida Kahlo. A stuffed monkey was pinned to her shoulder. She wore a thin white blouse and a long colorful skirt. She even had on rouge and lipstick. I noticed Maria by the door, hugging Ms. McGriff. Mexico Mendoza was back, and she looked like a movie star. Two braids were piled on top of her tiny head.

Both of her ears were showing.

"Mexico," Gorpat said. His eyes twinkled.

"Hi, Gorpat," she said, blushing. She did not look at me.

"Lylice, daaaaaaarling!" The girls flounced back over. Hannah stepped in front of Gorpat like he was invisible. "Oh . . . Mexico?"

Their mouths hung open in sneers. Hannah glared from me to Mexico. Debbie stared at Mexico's ear. "You're not supposed to be here. You're supposed to be in the hospital," she said.

"Hannah Anderson," I snapped, "obviously, she's *out* of the hospital!"

"Lylice, chill," Hannah said.

"Mexico, by any chance, would you care to dance?" Gorpat asked, elbowing past Hannah and holding out his four-fingered hand. Frodo led Frida onto the dance floor. Hannah made an ugly face behind Gorpat's back. Mr. S. was playing "Twist and Shout."

"No, I don't think I will chill, Hannah. Mexico

has nothing to do with me and Nathan coming to this stupid dance together anyway!"

"Well, he's in the bathroom," she said, as if I should have known. "And if he finds out Mexico's here, he's gonna be real upset. I'm going to tell him."

"Fine!"

My cheeks felt like lit matches. Maria now stood with Mrs. Lanza at the snack table. They smiled and looked out at Mexico and Gorpat. Hannah clunked back, almost tripping on her heel.

"Nathan wants to talk to you. Now. He says it's real important."

"Fine." I said. I followed her and Debbie out of the gym and into Ballot Hall.

"Go in. He's waiting!"

I pushed open the door to the boys' bathroom.

"Hello?" I coughed. They obviously hadn't cleaned this bathroom since my last visit. I plugged my nose. A thing with a long brown wig and fake arm tattoos stood before me. My penny loafers did not match his combat boots. Nor did my white gloves match his black eyeliner.

"Hey, Lylice."

"Nathan, it smells like urine. Who are you?"

"Ozzy Osbourne."

"Oh. He's famous, I guess. For eating rats."

Nathan laughed. "Bats," he said.

"Gross."

"Yeah," he said. "It is."

I wasn't in the mood for more standing around with Nathan Shelby while he said nothing. I wanted him to tell me why this had all happened. To tell me he was sorry.

"Nathan, you really did something mean," I said, wiping my tears away fast.

"I know," he said. Our eyes locked. "I . . . I, uh . . . I'm so sorry about Mexico." He swallowed. "It was all Hannah's idea. She talked me into it because . . . because she's mad at Mexico. But I'm not."

"How could she be mad at Mexico?" I asked. I remembered the way Hannah looked at Maria the night we dropped off the laundry.

"I don't know," he said, looking away. I sighed. "Lylice, I have something . . . to tell you," Nathan said.

I stood up straight. My heart started to pound, and my palms felt wet. He cleared his throat. "I, uh—I like—I *really* like your notes. And I like what you say. In class. Anywhere." He glanced at the door. "Everyone wishes they could say what you say."

More tears bubbled at the bottoms of my eyes. I brushed them away before they fell. Our faces were so close together that I could feel his breath on my nose.

And then he came even closer.

He took my hand.

"I can't . . . I can't be how you can be, Lylice. I'm sorry. But . . ." He closed his eyes and came toward me. He put his lips on top of mine and kissed me. There was a buzzing in my ears and my heart. My feet were outgrowing my shoes. Something was sucking all of the air out of my lungs.

Nathan Shelby was the most confusing boy in the whole world.

He took a step back and let go of my hand. For a second I was disappointed that I hadn't remembered to feel exactly how that hand felt against mine. But there was too much else happening. Would I ever remember? I opened my mouth and nothing came out but breath.

"I'm sorry," he said. "I'm not like you. I wish I was." He rubbed his twisted-up forehead. "Lylice, the truth is, if I tell anyone else that I really like you, they'll . . ." He swallowed again, and rubbed his forehead harder. "They won't like me."

His eyes pleaded for something. The smell of his warm breath faded into the stench of the boys' bathroom.

I stared into those blue eyes. All of the mean words his father said banged into my brain and I could not say the things *I* wanted to say. I *could not* say them. But something more than words took over. Without knowing it, without planning it, I raised my hand slowly. It came level with Nathan's face. And then a force that I couldn't control began to sizzle in my toes, and it zapped its way up my legs and into my gut and it burned my heart and my cheeks and then all of it, all of the strength of it, fused into my hand and—

Smack.

Nathan gasped. He put his hand on his cheek, and his mouth froze open. His eyes widened and his lips trembled. He nodded. And then he cried. Nathan Shelby, our sixth-grade class president, began to sob.

"I'm s-s-sorry. I'm an idiot."

He cried an old cry. One that had been waiting a long time to be let out. It made me feel like crying too.

Screeeech.

The door to the sprinkler closet burst open. I wheeled around.

Mike Black emerged, bounding into the bathroom holding a wrench. Under his overalls, he wore a red flannel shirt. His long ponytail wiggled through the back of a baseball cap. He stood between Nathan and me.

"Shelby," he said, shaking his head. "You're *such* a chicken."

Nathan wiped his nose. Eyeliner dripped down his face. A dark red mark had appeared on his left cheek.

Mike nodded at me once, solemnly, and headed to the door. "Shelby eats it!" he yelled. Then he was gone. Just as the door closed behind him, Hannah, Tony, and Debbie rushed in.

"Ohmigod!" said Hannah, gawking at Nathan, who stood against the stalls wiping his eyes.

Debbie gasped. Tony, wearing jeans, a sweater, and a pink Mohawk wig, whispered, "Bone."

Nathan sniffled.

Hannah walked right up to me. "We got you, Lylice," she said. "Nathan only said yes to you as a *dare*. He really wanted to come with *me*."

I couldn't catch Nathan's eye. He had faded away into the background of the scene, and Hannah had taken over. It dawned on me that he always let people take over.

"Gentlemen." I bowed to the boys. "Ladies." I curtsied. The only way to keep from crying was to be firm. "I do not wish to share any of your company from this point on. Ever. Ever. *Ever* again," I said. "Good night, and goodbye."

Hannah's sparkling eyes bored into me, her face hot red. I flung the door open and ran out.

"Lylice!" Principal Harrington, a vampire, met me right outside the door. "Now, what's going on? Who else is in there?"

I shrugged.

"Never mind. Just wait right inside the gym for me. I need to talk to you." He leaned in a little bit closer. "I want to know why Maria Mendoza is confirming her *appointment* with me for this Monday." He lowered his voice. "You knew I was interviewing secretaries. And it seems I've come up short on stacks of Susan B. Anthony stationery," he said, eyeing me. So he was playing detective. "Now, if I find out you had something to do with this, young lady, you're toast."

Harrington disappeared into the boys' bathroom. He was starting to sound like my dad. Great. Every time I thought I had a good idea, it backfired. Double great. I did not want to find out what becoming toast would entail. I supposed I could ask Mike Black for a debriefing.

Back in the gym, I spotted Mike, huddled in the haunted box with a group of boys (none were in costume). They all had their eyes on the ceiling. The dance floor was packed. "Funky Town" blared through Mr. S.'s speakers. The lioness and her tamer twirled and spun. Frodo and Frida were right next to them, holding hands and stepping from side to side. Mexico's dimples practically took up the whole gym. It was all meant to be. I deserved mine, and she hers. I stood flat against the wall and chewed my lip.

Harrington would find out that I hit Nathan. Waves of terror flooded my heart. I would be sent to a juvenile detention center for violent adolescents. It would go on my permanent record. My poor parents, who would do anything in the world for me, would have to pay millions of dollars in lawyer fees. Nathan's face would become disfigured. And Mexico would start spending so much time with Gorpat that she wouldn't *need* to forgive me.

The door connecting the gym to Ballot Hall flew open. Harrington burst in, shaking his head, clutching the back of Tony's neck with one hand and Nathan's with the other. They stumbled right past me and headed to the snack table. What had just happened?

"Leelas."

I turned around.

"Oh. Hi, Maria. You're still here."

Did Mexico tell her anything? Did she hate me? Could she tell that I had just been kissed?

My first kiss.

Maria hugged me tight. Mexico watched us from the dance floor. There was no smile in her eyes.

"Do you want to know what?" asked Maria, putting her hand over her heart. I nodded. "I am coming to interview on Monday to be the secretary here!" She blew her nose into a scrunched tissue. "Do you believe that?"

"Oh, Maria, that's really great," I said. It was, but my heart was so heavy that I couldn't muster up as much enthusiasm as I should have.

"Lylice!" Harrington's black cape arrived a second later than he did. He smiled through confusion. "Now, Ms. Mendoza tells me—"

"Oh, Principal Harrington, thank you thank you thank you!" She made the sign of the cross and then kissed her fingers.

"Yes, Miss Mendoza was just telling me that you've called her in to interview for the secretary position," I said.

"*Gracias,* Principal Harrington. I can't say it enough. *Muchas gracias* on behalf of myself, and" —she swallowed—"Mexico."

"I . . ." Harrington said.

"Oh, Leelas." Maria grabbed my hand. "Principal Harrington," she said, and grabbed his. "I can't thank you enough. You've both taken such good care of Mexico, and now me." She dabbed her eyes with her tissue.

"Hope you get the job," I said, waving and walking away. I had done *my* part. If Harrington dared tell that woman not to come in to interview, he could lump it.

I made my way to the dance floor. Streamers had fallen from the hoops, and half-eaten apples littered the gym floor. Harrington would've pulled me aside if he knew about what I did in the bathroom, right? He would've said something, right? A tinge of cool, guilty relief eased my heart. Was I actually *getting away* with assaulting a classmate?

I passed Nathan and Tony, who were sitting at the snack table. Aha. It must have come out somehow that *Tony* hit Nathan. They were both definitely being punished. Nathan held a baggie full of ice to his face. Tony playfully jabbed at his arm, but Nathan didn't seem to care. He looked miserable.

The black-cat cake was a platter of crumbs, and all the candy, even the sugar-free gummy worms and spiders, was gone. Hannah and Debbie were now huddled in the haunted box. Mike and his crew were nowhere to be found. Mr. S. announced the last dance of the evening. On my way to Mexico and Gorpat, he tapped me.

"Lylice, where've you been? Are you and Nathan havin' a super good time?"

"No, Mr. S.," I said. "No." I sighed. "The Hop's turned out to be a—a flop." My eyes watered.

"Lylice, I'm so sorry," he said. He bent down and whispered into my ear. "Between you, me, and the lamppost, Nathan Shelby is not . . . ready for you." He stood straight. "Now, why don'tcha get out there with Mexico and shake it!" He wiggled his hips from side to side and winked. I made it onto the dance floor with no intention of shaking it.

"Hello, Miss Anthony. Having a good time?" asked Gorpat.

"No. Goodbye, Frodo." I bowed to him. I faced Mexico. She looked away. She took Gorpat's hand and they started to sway to "Happy Trails to You." I couldn't breathe. Mexico Mendoza did not want anything to do with me.

I headed to the snack table to find my picket signs.

Tony's jabs had become playful punches. Nathan was still not fighting back.

"Quit," said Nathan. Tony snickered and socked Nathan in the arm. A small group of kids watched. Harrington's whistle blew.

"I said *quit,* Tony!" And then Nathan lunged for Tony, who fell backward. "Happy Trails" ended.

Sploosh!

Good thing Mrs. Lanza's metal bucket, full of cold water and apples, was there to catch Tony's fall.

"Yipes, it's freezing!" Then Tony yelped a word that started with *F.*

The entire school stared in silence. Tony Frizell smacked his hand over his mouth. Kids looked at one another with smiling eyes and open jaws. Was it wrong to feel relief? My offense in the boys' bathroom was definitely dwarfed by Tony's use of the F-word while floating in a bucket.

Harrington grabbed a sopping Tony by the arm and barked into his ear. Tony's Mohawk had slipped down onto his cheek, making it look as if he had one pink sideburn. Teachers started shepherding people toward the front of the gym.

I darted past Nathan, who sat with his head in his hands, and grabbed my picket signs from under the snack table. They now read DON'T BE A DOLT, GET OUT AND SMOKE and WOMAN AND MAN, LET'S MAKE A BABY.

Just then, the lights flickered. Students screamed. Teachers shushed. Wisps of water spat from the ceiling. It was raining in the Susan B. Anthony Middle School gym. Light showers fell toward the back at first, right on top of Debbie and Hannah in the haunted box. Then the entire ceiling poured water.

Kids would not stop screaming and laughing. Someone flung Sari Henderson's cardboard torch across the gym. Masks and empty paper cups were hurled into the air. More yelling. Louder laughing.

Harrington's whistle screeched. My ears burned. He yelled for everyone to remain calm. That we were acting like monkeys in a zoo. Coach Zito barked that people should relax, it was only a little water. Mrs. Lanza was doing her best to shield several students from the downpour under her sorceress's cape. The lights flickered again.

Blackout.

Students screeched and howled to the moon. Helium balloons popped. Smells of soggy cardboard, toilet water, apple juice, and bubblegum seemed stronger in the dark. Elbows and hands pushed against me from all directions.

Harrington blew and blew and blew his whistle. And blew it some more. He opened the door of the gym that connects to Ballot Hall, letting a ray of light into the wet blackness. We were ordered to file out immediately. The lights flickered and came on again. I searched for Mike but didn't see him anywhere.

For the first time all night, I smiled.

Soon the hallway of Ballot Hall was jammed with wet Susan B. Anthony Middle School students. I squished my way through the crowd, stumbled down the Ballot Hall steps, and found my dad waiting in the parking lot.

"What happened?" he asked as I plopped into the front seat after throwing my vandalized picket signs into the back.

"Nothing, " I said, and I began pulling out bobby pins, releasing the bun and letting my hair fall into my face.

"Lily-bean, why are you crying?" my dad asked gently.

"I'm not," I said. With a tissue from the glove box, I rubbed and rubbed the pink off my lips. "Mexico and Gorpat danced," I said, trying to catch my breath. I hoped Mexico would remember what it felt like to hold Gorpat's hand.

"Bean, why are you all wet?"

"And Maria Mendoza is interviewing at the school on Monday." My nose dripped.

"That's incredible, Lylice. I didn't even know . . . What is wrong?"

"And Nathan Shelby . . ." I rolled down my window. Gnawed on my lip. We stopped at a red light.

"And Nathan Shelby kissed me in the boys' bathroom," I whispered.

"Lily-bean." My father's eyes were smiling.

"Daddy, are you *laughing?*" I reeled around and glared at him.

"I'm not! I'm sorry. The boys' bathroom?"

"Never mind. It was all a disaster." Tears drenched my hoop skirt. The cool night slipped into the car through my open window.

"I'm sorry, Lily-bean. I'm sorry. Boys are bad

news. Know what I mean, Bean?" I watched the light turn from red to green. Both colors got all fuzzy with the water in my eyes.

We rode the rest of the way home in silence. All of the things that Nathan liked about me were the same things that made him have to pretend not to.

THE SUFFRAGETTE STAR

VOLUME 5

SPRINKLER OR SKINWALKER?

by Lylice Martin, Staff Writer

Double, double, toil and . . . rain?

Wait a minute. Rain?

Yes, fellow students. The highlight of this year's Halloween Sock Hop was not Mrs. Lanza's sorcerer costume, nor was it Mrs. Schvitter's jammin' tunes, or the German chocolate black cat cake. According to Susan B. Anthony Middle School students, the best part of the dance came toward the end of the evening, when streams of water rained down on us in the gym.

At approximately 9:45 p.m. small, mysterious sprinkles fell from the ceiling. Moments later, there was a downpour and a blackout. Luckily, no one was injured. But all were drenched!

This roving reporter caught up with several students at lunch the Monday after the incident.

"I think Harrington probably planned it. To scare us," said sixth-grader Tony Frizell, flopping fries into a pool of ketchup. "Me likey!"

"It was odd," said Gorpat Geetha, seventh grade, while collecting aluminum cans from tables for the school's recycling bin. "Unexpected. Very Halloween."

So what caused the showers?

Principal Harrington did not return our e-mail for comment.

The gym is closed for the remainder of the quarter, so tennis has been canceled for the rest of the week.

"*Yo no se,*" said Senora Schwartz after Spanish. "One minute I'm doing the merengue, the next minute I'm a dripping mess! *Ay yi yi!* Probably just a problem with the sprinkler valve."

But was it just a sprinkler malfunction?

Readers, remember that it was Halloween. And we live in the Southwest, where Native American folklore and tradition might just be true and living among us! If you've never heard of the term "Skinwalker," you should look it up online (if you like getting spooked!). Skinwalkers are a group of Navajo medicine persons that can change from humans to any animal they want.

Picture this: it's the night of the hop. The teachers and student leaders are busy setting up the gym. Snacks are set and jack-o'-lanterns are lit. Somehow, a Skinwalker sneaks into the school, in the form of a camel. Just for a joke. After all, it's Halloween! Remember that camels can store twenty gallons of water in their humps. At just the right moment, the camel sneaks into the gym and spits gallons and gallons on our heads!

The witchcraft that was brewing at our sock hop gave us all a nice, refreshing Halloween scare!

Log on to:

http://nogalesflowers.blogspot.com

to post your Halloween Hop rain reaction, *and to sign an important petition!*

A Promise Is a Promise

Hannah and Nathan were now officially boyfriend and girlfriend. Debbie and Tony were too. Tony and Nathan had been given detention every day after school for a week. I heard that Harrington didn't even let them explain, that he took one look and dragged them both out of that bathroom. And rumor had it that after the dance, Harrington forced Tony Frizell to tell his mother *himself* what he'd said in the bucket. Bone.

The gym was off limits until further notice.

Mike was suspended. Indefinitely. I hoped Harrington would let him back into school soon and that he wouldn't give up on him.

In the eyes of the Susan B. Anthony Middle School

administration, I hadn't hit anyone at the Halloween Sock Hop. I wasn't proud of losing my temper, just relieved I avoided my fifth detention in one quarter. No teachers pulled me aside. I didn't receive any disapproving looks. Principal Harrington did not call me into his office for questioning.

He was preoccupied, what with training his new damn secretary, Maria Mendoza! On Friday morning, her first day, I peeked into the supply office before English and found her making copies. She told me that her contract would help her renew her visa, and that health insurance would be just around the corner.

"Miss Mendoza, that's the best news I've heard all quarter," I said.

"Me too," she said, smiling. Mexico and I hadn't spoken in exactly one week. I wondered if she'd told her aunt anything. "Get along to class, *chica,*" she chirped. "We'll talk later."

During second period, we played fruit charades *en español.* I tried to find Mexico's eyes while she was acting out *naranja,* but she wouldn't look at me. I remembered Mexico on the first day of school, holding her backpack so tight, hardly talking. Watching her at the front of the room pretending to bite into a sour orange and making the whole class laugh made me long so much to be her friend again. But she was different now, and maybe she didn't need me.

After the bell, I walked up to Señora's desk, slowly, trying to time it so that everyone would leave before I got there.

"*Qué pasa,* Concepción?" she asked cheerfully.

"Señora, this is long overdue, but I wanted to—to apologize for—*destruir.* From before? I never gave you this." I opened my brain-on-wheels and handed her the Frida Kahlo poster.

"Oh, Concepción," she said, unrolling the poster. "Ahhh, Señorita Kahlo," she said, hugging me. *"Muchas gracias. Es mi día de suerte!"* She gave me a squeeze.

I noticed a sandwich baggie full of notes on her desk. My mouth fell open. Then I cleared my throat.

"Señora . . . um . . ." How did I say this? "Are those the notes that were confiscated from Juanita?"

She glanced at them and nodded. "*Sí. La Señorita* Anderson *no es muy astuta, eh?* She is not so sly, is she, Concepción?"

204

"No," I mumbled. "She isn't."

Señora raised and lowered her eyebrows lots of times in a row, grinning. "So, what about those notes?" Her voice was quieter now, and she stood with her hand on her hip, looking me right in the eyes.

"Well . . . the situation is . . . they're mine. I wrote them," I said. I bit my lip. "T-to Pedro."

Señora handed me those notes. I stared at her pink sandals. I stood for a second longer, wanting her to say something else, but I didn't know what.

"Okay, Concepción, it's okay. Bye-bye, *señorita. Hasta luego,*" she said, giving me another, tighter squeeze.

"Hasta luego, Señora," I said, bending down to shove the baggie into my brain-on-wheels. "Thank you."

Sadness and relief flooded through me as I hurried out of the room and headed to social studies. The notes had made it back to their author.

"All righty, sports fans," said Coach Zito, "you may whisper among yourselves for the next five minutes, and then it's off to the cafeteria for announcements. Oh, and we had one student turn in some very cre-

205

ative extra-credit this quarter." Coach searched his desk. Heads turned toward me. Eyes rolled. I stared forward. *Don't look at me,* I wanted to say. I slouched in my seat.

"Mexico Mendoza made this," he said, holding up a picture of Arizona, "and I wanted to show it off." He nodded at Mexico, whose cheeks and neck turned pink.

I sat up straight, straining to see the project. If you looked at it closer, Arizona was the body of a person. It had dark brown hair. Two little legs sprang from the bottom, and arms came out the sides. One ear was smaller than the other. Where its heart should be was a tiny drawing of Mexico, the country. Butterflies danced inside it.

There were words written with different colored pencils all over Arizona. *Bear Mountain. Tucson. Tuba. Conquistadores.*

I melted as I studied Mexico's picture. She probably didn't even need me as an English Buddy anymore. She was doing great in school without me. I was tired of trying to be so smart and figure things out all the time, and have all the answers. Some people didn't try so hard, and they seemed to know more. Seemed to do more.

If Mrs. Garrison hadn't decided that I could handle sixth grade, or if Mr. Harrington had sent me back to fifth, I might have been the smartest person at Catalina Elementary. But even though I was not turning out to be the smartest, or the best at anything, I would rather be here. Because here was where Mexico was. And maybe I still had a chance.

"All righty, to the cafeteria we go," Coach said.

The yellow lunch table buzzed around Nathan and Hannah, who sometimes held hands and who had supposedly kissed in the alley behind the school. Ha. Just *how many* girls had Nathan Shelby kissed? Preposterous. And gross.

Boys *were* bad news. They were rats in pants and shirts scampering around, the jerks. I avoided Nathan like smallpox. I somehow felt his blue eyes searching me out all week, just to check in, but I had not allowed them the satisfaction. I got my French bread pizza combo and headed for the red table. Tony and a group of boys passed by me.

"It's *bone,* dude! My grandma's coming for the

whole week and staying in *my room*," Tony was saying. "What the crap, right?"

The red table was empty. I was about to sit when *tap tap tap* went someone's fingers on my shoulder. I turned around.

"*Hola,*" said Mexico. Gorpat stood behind her. "Can we sit with you?"

I nodded, my heart pounding.

Mexico and I were back our table, along with Gorpat. Principal Harrington and Miss Mendoza had set up the PA system. He formally introduced her as the new school secretary. She waved to everyone, and the school clapped. Harrington spoke about striving for excellence in the next quarter, and then introduced the teachers. Some had special awards to give out.

Mexico got one from Ms. McGriff for "Top Tuba Tackler." Gorpat was awarded "Blue-Ribbon Reader of the Quarter" from Mrs. Lanza. And Tony got the "Best Volleys" award from Coach. Hoping I would get something seemed small. After all, Mexico had spoken to me.

Sari Henderson announced eighth-grade honor roll for the quarter, and then Gorpat Geetha announced it for seventh grade. When Nathan approached the microphone to announce sixth-grade honor roll, boys yelled, "Nate-o!" and girls chanted, "Swellby Shelby! Swellby Shelby!"

"Hi, students."

He read the names. I had made it. What was better, *Mexico Mendoza* had made it, even after she had missed so much school. I threw both fists up into the air without thinking and whispered: "Yes!"

Me and Miss Mendoza and Mexico had all promised to climb Bear Mountain if this happened. I sighed. Could we still do it?

"We will now announce Trailblazer Award nominations," said Harrington.

"What?" I croaked. "They're announcing that today?" I whispered.

Gorpat nodded, biting his nails.

"The Susan B. Anthony Trailblazer Award is given annually, in the spring," Harrington declared, "to one student from any grade who excels in academics, extracurricular activities, and who is highly respected by his or her peers."

The cafeteria held its breath.

"I will now announce the nominees. Hold your applause, please. The nominees are . . ." Harrington unfolded a piece of paper. I think I heard twenty pins drop.

"Eighth-grader Sari Henderson. Seventh-grader Gorpat Geetha. And for sixth grade"—Harrington grinned—"we have a tie this year."

He paused.

"Sixth-graders Lylice Martin and Nathan Shelby."

Everyone went wild. The yellow table chanted, "Swellby Shelby! Swellby Shelby!" Students clapped and screamed. Harrington's whistle blew four times. Then lunch began, officially.

Gorpat and I leaned in and smiled past Mexico at each other. With one hand on Gorpat's shoulder and one on mine, Mexico said, "Two best nominees."

The Trailblazer Award? It didn't really hit me.

"So, Mexico, by any chance, can I give you a call later tonight?" Gorpat asked, taking a bite of pizza.

"Well, I think . . . I think I am going to Leelas's tonight." She beamed at me. "But you can call me tomorrow," she said.

"I will." Gorpat blushed. The three of us ate together, quickly, as lunch was cut short due to announcements.

"Congratulations on your nomination, Gorpat," I said.

"You too, Lylice," he said, grinning.

"Mexico . . ." I didn't know what to say. I sighed. "How's your B.S.?"

"One hundred," she said. I nodded.

We sat another minute.

"How is Meatball?" she asked.

"Still peeing in the heat vent."

She smiled. The red in Gorpat's cheeks deepened.

"Mexico, do you want to sleep over?"

"I got honor roll. And we have Bear Mountain," said Mexico. "A promise is a promise."

A Note from a Boy

I could not stop smiling. I didn't care about my teeth, what I looked like, who I was to anyone but Mexico. She and Gorpat grinned at me. It is when you have friends that you are beautiful. I thought of Mike Black, and half wished he hadn't been suspended, but half admired the stunt that he had pulled.

Before I could prepare myself, Nathan was standing in front of the red table.

"Hey," he said. The look Mexico gave him could have frozen the Tucson sun.

"Good morning, Nathan. What can we do for you?" I asked in my most professional voice. Nathan stared at his pants.

"Congratulations, Nate," said Gorpat.

"You too," said Nathan.

No one spoke. Suddenly Gorpat said he needed to return a book to Mrs. Lanza. He said goodbye and walked off. Gorpat was the smartest boy I knew.

"Hi, Mexico," Nathan said. She finished her carrots and scrunched her paper bag as if no one had spoken to her.

"Uh, I wanted to say—congratulations, Lylice."

"Thank you."

I stared at Nathan with my eyebrows raised. Mexico was scowling at him. He drummed his fingers on his khakis.

"Nate-o!" Tony yelled from the yellow table while whapping a squealing Debbie with French fries. "Come here!" Hannah called, "Swellby Shelby!" Nathan glanced at them, and then looked back at me.

"Lylice." He sighed. He reached into his pocket, pulled out a note, and set it on the red table. Then he was gone. I could not speak.

"Leelas," Mexico said, snatching the note. "Not now. After school."

I nodded. She was right. What would I do after reading this? Nathan's words were in Mexico's hand.

She carried a secret piece of him with her for the rest of the day. I was half ecstatic and half nauseated. In math, we played times-tables trivia, and during band, Ms. McGriff put on *West Side Story*. I love the scene where brave Anita faces all the Jet hoodlums, but my mind was elsewhere. After school, my brain-on-wheels and I clanked down the Ballot Hall steps as Harrington trudged up them.

"Oh, Principal Harrington, sir, I have something for you," I said. Harrington looked pooped. He smiled and waited.

I had debated whether or not to give it to him. But it seemed the right thing to do. After all, what would I do with it? It wasn't my dad's style. I opened my suitcase and handed him the thin box.

"It's a gift to say thank you for welcoming me to the school," I said. "And to apologize . . . for everything. I won't behave like a monkey in a zoo next quarter."

"Aw, Lylice, now, this is unnecessary." Harrington shook his head. He lifted the lid.

"An orange bow tie?" A smile overtook his face. "This is *beautiful,* Lylice. Thank you. Thank you very much." He shook and shook my hand and grinned and grinned. "Very much. Very, very much," he said again. It wasn't cheap, but my dad helped me out.

"You're welcome. You should start a collection," I offered. Harrington smiled. "Have a good weekend," I called, clanking down the next step.

"You too, Lylice. Thank you again for this." He held up the box. "So very thoughtful of you." He waved and then straightened his red bow tie. "And, Lylice," he called. "Relax now, you and Mexico. Won't ya? Just relax."

"Oh, we'll try to," I said. "But we probably won't."

"Mr. Harrington?" Miss Mendoza rushed down the steps to meet us. "I finished. We can put your things back on your desk Sunday, when the paint is dry. I hope you like it. Do you need me to check the in-box, or any of those kind of things—"

"Thanks, Maria, no. You can leave early this afternoon. Have a good weekend. And thank you. Can't wait to see my new desk."

Now that Miss Mendoza was around, I was sure his heart would start aching for Art Attack soon enough. I made up my mind right there that over fall break, Mexico and I would scheme up some new plans. I could see big changes coming. An art club. A real, outside tennis court. We'd help Harrington find the funds. Maybe we could even make it an official rule that a *student* editor be the last one to check the word count in the *Suffragette Star* before it came out. Excitement filled me as I wondered about the next quarter of school.

"Oh, *gracias,* Principal Harrington!" As Maria hugged him, I noticed his shoulders drop from his ears. "Leelas, I'll pick you girls up tomorrow morning, with my hiking boots on!"

She dashed down to the Great Lawn. Harrington smiled at me, then shook his head. I waved at him. Maybe next quarter Harrington and I could figure out how to go over that weird bridge *together* instead of always needing to get out of each other's way.

As I lugged my brain-on-wheels down the rest of the steps, I watched Miss Mendoza head toward the parking lot. I caught up with Mexico and Gorpat on the Great Lawn.

"Well, by any chance, would you mind if my parents and I meet you at Bear Mountain?" Gorpat was saying. "We're going tomorrow too."

"Yes! That will be good," Mexico said, smiling.

"Good. Congratulations again on your tuba prize. Bye. Bye, Lylice."

"Bye, Gorpat," I said. "And may the best Trailblazer win!" He grinned and nodded.

"Bye." Mexico waved. Her nose wrinkled and her dimples were deeper than ever. "Come on, Leelas. Your dad," she said, grabbing my arm.

"It's Mexico Mendoza, my favorite Double M!" my dad said as Mexico and I squished into the front seat. "We're so darn glad to have you back. You're sleeping over, I hope," he said. Mexico nodded.

"Guess what, Mr. Martin, Leelas got nominated for the Trailblazer Award!" she said.

"Holy moly, Lil! That's so cool!" my dad said.

"Thanks, Dad. Well, you should see the extra-credit art piece Mexico did for Coach." Mexico blushed. I went on. "She also got an award from Ms. McGriff, *and* she made honor roll."

"What say we make pizzas tonight to celebrate?"

We nodded. "Yes, and—" Mexico stopped. Her mouth hung open.

My dad turned his head to the left and stared.

I strained my neck to see. Two cars down from us, something was happening. A big happening. We weren't the only ones gawking.

Hannah Anderson leaned against the trunk of her car, staring at the ground. JJ stood next to her, holding her hand and crying. But that was not the happening.

The happening was that Maria and Mrs. Anderson stood outside of the driver's-side door of the Andersons' fancy blue car and they were . . . fighting? Maria was definitely wrestling something from Mrs. Anderson's hand. Something that Mrs. Anderson didn't want to give up.

My dad turned off the car, threw open his door, and climbed out. Mexico and I just sat. Forgetting about politeness, I leaned over the driver's seat and rolled down the window.

"No!" Maria shouted. She had Hannah's mom's car keys in her hand and brought them up to Mrs. Anderson's face. *"No."*

Hannah's mom took off her sunglasses. Her hair was all messy. She glanced around the Great Lawn and wiped her eyes. Even though she was two cars away, I could tell she was crying.

"I'm driving," said Maria. She made Hannah and JJ get in the back seat. Then she helped Mrs. Anderson to the passenger side and opened the door. Mrs. Anderson almost fell into the car. Maria walked back around to the driver's side.

Mexico and I didn't move. I don't think we were breathing either. My dad held Maria's hands and said something that we could not hear. Maria nodded and said something to him and then bent down and looked at Mexico and me. She blew us a kiss. Then she got into the fancy blue car and drove away with the Andersons.

My dad got in our car, and nobody talked the whole way home.

"Double M, your aunt is a saint," my dad said as we turned into our driveway.

Mexico looked scared.

"Daddy, where's Maria taking Hannah's mom?" I asked. He stared straight ahead and sighed.

"Girls, Hannah's mom's . . . sick."

"You mean an alcoholic?" I asked.

"Yes," my dad said. He shifted in his seat. "And Maria's just driving her home for now. And she's talk-

ing about getting Hannah's mom on a bus to Sedona."
He fiddled with the rearview mirror. "There's a really
good . . . hospital there."

"You mean a rehabilitation center?"

"Yes," he said. "Mexico, you don't mind staying
with us for the weekend, do you?" he asked, glancing
at us out of the corner of his eye. Mexico's lips made
a smile, but it didn't look like she meant it. I took her
hand.

"Maria'll call us tomorrow," my dad said. "Don't
worry. Don't you worry at all."

Once inside, Mexico and I headed to my room and
she took out Nathan's note. We sat on my bed. A
note from a boy was a big deal. His words were in my
room.

But I have started to question big deals.

A Real Friend

"I feel bad for Hannah," Mexico said.

"Me too."

We didn't say anything else for a minute.

"Leelas," Mexico said, standing up. "Let us read." She unfolded the note. I fell back and lay on my bed, covering my ears.

"No matter what it says, that boy is bad," Mexico confirmed, clearing her throat. The smell of rising pizza dough floated into my room, and Mexico's stomach growled. We both giggled.

"'Leelas,'" she began reading, and then stopped. "Leelas, the handwriting is so bad."

"Mexico, just read!"

"Sorry!"

"'Leelas,'" she began again. "'I think you deserve

the Trailblazer Award more than anyone. From, Nate. P.S. Sorry.'"

I sat up. She joined me on the bed. We both stared forward.

"That's it?" I said, after a minute. Mexico sighed.

I blurted everything out.

Nathan kissing me, Mike Black in the closet, Hannah saying it was all a dare.

Mexico nodded and listened the whole time. It was like she had never even been mad. I told her I'd slapped Nathan. "I'm awful," I said.

"No, you aren't," Mexico said, shaking her head slowly, her eyes becoming tiny slits.

"But," I said, "he just cried. Nathan Shelby cried right there in front of me in the boys' bathroom." If *my* dad had told me I was an idiot before the dance, I would've wanted to cry too.

"Leelas," said Mexico, "that boy is still bad."

We plopped onto the floor and decided to dump out my brain-on-wheels and Mexico's backpack. Soon, piles of papers, pens, and grime littered my room. I dragged my garbage can over and we started throwing away old stuff. I'd recycle it later.

"Soup's on!" my dad called, knocking on my bedroom door. The smell of tomato sauce filled our noses. He brought in this big tray of food.

Before we ate, Mexico went and unzipped the small pocket of her backpack.

"Do you mind if I do it in here?" she asked, holding up the pen that said *Humalog*. I shook my head. I tried not to watch her as she pulled up her red blouse and stuck the pen right into her stomach. After a few seconds, she pulled it out. Then put it back in her backpack and smiled at me.

Mexico was going to be okay. And it was all because of the *Conquistadores*.

My dad's dinner tasted perfect. A wheat pizza with mushrooms, carrot and celery sticks, and sugar-free cream soda.

Mexico said that Gorpat had called her every night since the dance.

"You're sure you don't mind if he comes with us tomorrow?" she asked.

"The more the merrier," I said, slurping the last of the fizz at the bottom of my soda. She smiled as she finished her third piece. After dinner, I showed Mexico the sandwich baggie from Señora.

"So these are my notes to Nathan," I said, holding

223

it against my chest. "Señora gave them back to me."
I opened the bag to examine them.

"Oh, Leelas," she said, grabbing the bag and throwing it onto the garbage heap. "That boy didn't deserve those notes."

"Maybe you're right," I said.

"Hey," she said, her dimples coming out. "What were your other two Spanish verbs for Señora's project?" She climbed up on my bed, slid off her white sandals, and drew her knees up under her.

"I completely forgot about that!" I said. Mexico always knew the exact right thing to say. "As you recall, I had . . ." I grabbed a piece of scrap paper from the floor. Ripped it in half. And in half again. Again.

"Destruir!" Mexico shouted.

"Sí!" I said, pointing to her. I sprinkled all but one little ripped piece onto the floor and held it up. "This is a ballot, okay?"

Mexico squinted, looked up at my canopy, and then nodded. Grabbing a pen, I scribbled on the paper, and then folded it.

"Votar!" she yelled.

"Sí! And my last one was . . ." I marched to her,

put my arms around her, and squeezed.

"*Abrazar,*" she said, squeezing back. We giggled and giggled and then sat back down on the floor. The first quarter of school lay in front of us in a heap.

"I guess I should get a big black garbage sack," I said. She nodded. Meatball was curled up near her, licking Mexico's toes.

"Mexico," I said, examining the note bag again. "I know it's silly to keep these, but . . ." I opened a note.

It was handwritten, not typed.

There was a message at the top in curlicue hand-writing, and then a messy printed response at the bottom.

Definitely not my note.

"Oh my God."

"What! What?" she asked.

My jaw dropped. I opened another. Same thing. Curly at the top, messy at the bottom.

"Oh my God!" I spoke too quickly. "The-notes-that-Señora-confiscated-from-Hannah. They weren't mine." I gulped. "They were *hers.*"

"Huh?" Mexico's forehead wrinkled.

"Mexico," I said, slowing down. "These notes are all between *Hannah and Nathan*." I swallowed, taking in what this meant: a private look into Hannah Anderson. Shame snuck into a feeling of absolute satisfaction.

I fell back onto my bed. My brain hurt. Mexico cleared her throat and stood up. I tossed the bag into her outstretched hands. More of Nathan was in my room. A whole lot more. I covered my eyes.

She began the first one.

> Dear Nathan, JJ loooves you and Tony. So does my mom and Steve. Steve is like really new but my mom is so into him. Something about him . . .

"Leelas, there are hearts all over this," Mexico whined.

"Just read," I ordered. "Please."

> Something about him weirds me out. Maria thinks so too. And she is the

only one my mom really listens to. So
hopefully he won't be there next time
you guys come over. Anyways, meet me
in the alley after school. XO, Han

Nathan wrote at the bottom:

Hannah, See you after school.
From, Nate
P.S. That guy Steve offered me
a cigarette. I didn't take it!

Meatball's coarse tongue kissed my thumb.
Nathan had gone to Hannah's? What else didn't I
know about? My heart pounded. Mexico unfolded
the next note.

Dear Nathan, My mom didn't hear
you leave. No surprise. Once I stayed
at Deb's for two nights instead of
one and when I got home she forgot
I was even gone at all. That was
really nice of you to come over and

cheer me up. Sorry about the yelling.
XO, Han

Nathan wrote back:

Hannah, You're very welcome.
The yelling wasn't bad. You
should come to my house.
From, Nate

Meatball crawled on top of my chest, purring.
Mexico read the next one.

Dear Nathan, You are turning out to
be my best friend this year. Even Deb
doesn't know about all that stuff. I
hate Maria for quitting. Did you know
that when she figured everything out
she told me she would stay and help
my mom? But she didn't. She couldn't
handle it. Nobody ever can. Now . . .

Mexico's eyes were watering. She sat down next
to me and continued reading.

228

> Now everything is worse. Anyways,
> you should go with me to that
> stupid dance. It's going to be stupid
> anyways. Just because your dad asked
> you to be friends with Lylice this
> year doesn't mean you have to go
> with her. She's a loser. And I know
> you want to go with me. Alley after
> school and we'll figure it out. XO, Han

Mexico let out a breath. I felt her glance at me, but I didn't look at her.

> Hannah, Sorry about all that
> stuff. I guess I would rather
> go with you. See you after
> school. From, Nate
> P.S. Just so you know, I would
> have been friends with Lylice
> anyway.

Scritch scritch scratch went Meatball at her post. From down the hall, the TV buzzed. My blue bed screeked as Mexico changed position beside me.

So Hannah and Nathan were best friends. They could talk about things that I didn't know about. That was just the way it was.

We stared forward.

Crack.

Thunder outside? Meatball's ears pricked up and she hopped back onto the bed. It never rains in Arizona. Me and Mexico leaned back and lay on our backs under the blue. I let out a huge sigh. She shifted onto her side and rested her palm on her cheek.

"Mexico, do you think my canopy is babyish?" I asked suddenly.

"I always wanted to have a canopy," she said.

We lay there for a while.

"I can't be*lieve* she said she hates your—" I started to say.

"Leelas," Mexico interrupted, "just ignore it." She was right. The more I thought about it, the less I disliked Hannah. And the more I felt sad for her. Mexico knew what people were made of before she got to know them. It was as if we were all packages of unmarked seeds, and she knew what flowers we'd be before we unfolded.

"Maybe," said Mexico after a minute. She patted

Meatball, who pawed at a pillow. "Maybe that boy is not *so* bad."

Meatball purred. We both scratched behind one of her ears, and her eyes fell closed. Rain usually skips over Tucson and goes down into the Gulf of Mexico. But tonight we were lucky. I kneeled and muscled open my window. We could see Nathan's trampoline getting soaked.

The rain rumbled down. Mike Black popped into my head, and I grinned. I longed to talk to him. The letter from Mrs. BlackBear that I was never meant to see was tucked into a cubby in my desk, along with the gift I'd meant to give Mexico.

In the boys' bathroom, Mike had said that Nathan was a chicken. I wanted to tell him that *I* was a chicken. I didn't deserve to be here with Mexico now. After everything that had happened.

"Mexico," I said, breaking the silence, "when you fainted that day, what did it feel like?"

She lay back with her arms folded under her head, gazing into the blue. "I don't remember," she said, after a minute. "The only thing I know"—she swallowed—"is I was thinking of my mom when I woke up."

Meatball purred in the silence.

"Why did they . . . name you Mexico?" I asked. She didn't answer. I felt a moment of panic. What was it of my business? Why did I need to know?

"It's okay," she whispered. "My mom wanted me to born in her city. Nogales, Mexico. She could have come here for better medicine and those kind of things, but she didn't. She died . . . when I was born. But she wanted me to born in Mexico. I think she would like it: me, Mexico."

The raindrops quieted down. Wet desert air blew at my curtains, which billowed. Mexico and I lay side by side in our imitation Juicies.

"Leelas?"

"Yeah?"

Mexico stared into the canopy.

"Even if . . . even if my mom was somebody like Hannah's mom, I still wish I could have known her."

I grabbed her hand. Squeezed. She squeezed back. I slipped off the bed, shuffled through my desk, and found the small box.

"It's from when you were sick. I brought it to the hospital that one day, but you were so tired," I said, handing it to her.

I chewed on my lip as she lifted the cotton and pulled out the necklace. It had a gold chain, and the butterfly charm was red and gold. A big smile stretched her cheeks wide. She sat up straight, bowed her head, and reached behind her neck to put it on. "I love it," she said. "Thank you, Leelas."

"Welcome. It'll match your barrettes."

Her eyes started to water and she nodded. Mexico studied me. I let her. I looked right back at her, but didn't study. She took in my brown eyes, my cheeks, my big teeth, my questions. She glanced around my room. My eyes followed hers. Meatball. The tray of empty plates and glasses. My brain-on-wheels. And I could feel her loving it all. Again. But it felt wrong. I had lied to her.

"Mexico," I said, swallowing and trying to get the words out. "That painting you made me? I left it that day . . . because it was meant for a *real* friend."

She climbed off the bed and kneeled down. Unzipped her backpack, pulled out her painting, and put it in my hands.

"Yes," she said. "You."

Next to Mexico

Mexico, Gorpat, and I make it to the top of Bear Mountain.

Saguaro cacti greet us, waving boldly. In November, Tucson air is wetter than in summer, so the blue flax, prickly pears, and chollas get more moisture. Fall is the best time to visit.

Wait, is that Mike Black? Yes! Mike Black is coming up from another trail, and he spots us. I've never seen his hair all down, falling on his shoulders like that. He nods at me, once, and smiles. We all stand looking out.

Mexico gazes, blinking. We see the Catalina Parkway winding to town. Catalina Foothills Elementary School. Cherryvale. Susan B. Anthony Middle

School. Highway 10, curving around and up, heading to Sedona. We are stars looking down at Earth.

Gorpat grins, pointing. Because we can see Mexico from the top.

Even though stars are billions of light-years away from one another, some can collide. Then they stay separate, but both become bigger.

Better.

Brighter, with little sparkling pieces of each other.

I am quiet, smiling.

Because I am standing next to Mexico.

Thank You

Thank you to my editor, Erica Zappy, for her enthusiasm and wisdom; without her this book would not be in your hands right now! Enormous thanks to all of my incredible friends and colleagues who encouraged me to continue writing this book, especially Micaela Blei, Brie-Anne Coker, Dorothy Cury, Liza Domnitz, Amy Fitts, Judy Gitenstein, Wendy Herlich, Ronnie Herman, Derek Moreno, David Silverman, Eileen Stevens, and Heidi Verhaal and her fifth grade class at the International School of the Peninsula.

Special thanks to Kim Prentice and Leigh Siegel-Czarkowski for answering my questions about diabetes, *y muchas gracias a Chachis Salazar Verhaal, Cameron Verhaal, y Marirosa Mia Garcia por ayudarme con mi español.*

Much thanks to all the Golds for their support. Thank you to my sister, Nancy West, and brother-in-law, Roger, for their honesty. Most of all, thank you to my parents, Frank and June Nails, for everything. To my dear husband, Mike Gold, thank you for your humor, your patience, and your love.